Helena Smole

Vivvy and Izzy the Dwarf: A series about relationships

Book 1:

Out of the Forest and into the City

A Fantasy Novel

Helena Smole
Vivvy and Izzy the Dwarf: A series about relationships
Book 1: Out of the Forest and into the City
A Fantasy Novel

Cover Illustration by Leon Zuodar.
English Language Editing by Dean J. DeVos.
Cover Design and Typesetting by Miha Bercko.
Published by Domen Smole, Škofja Loka, Slovenia, Europe. 2017. POD.

CIP - Kataložni zapis o publikaciji
Narodna in univerzitetna knjižnica, Ljubljana

821.163.6-312.9

SMOLE, Helena, 1974-
   Vivvy and Izzy the dwarf : a series about relationships : a fantasy novel. Book 1, Out of the forest and into the city / Helena Smole. - Škofja Loka : [published by D. Smole], 2017

ISBN 978-961-283-663-4

285062912

PRAISE FOR
Vivvy and Izzy the Dwarf:
A series about relationships – Book 1

"This is one of the most unusual approaches I have seen in the writing of a fantasy romance novel. Izzy, the Dwarf has access to many magical interventions that he could have used to assist the couple in their life journey. Instead, he consults with the wizards and turns that advice around to where the couple must figure out their issues on their own. Vivvy and Felix are on a journey of self-discovery. They are forced to come to grips with their childhood, how they feel about each other, and even their friendship with Izzy." – **Colleen M. Chesebro**, author of *The Heart Stone Chronicles - The Swamp Fairy*

"This book was a complete joy to read! The depth of the characters & plot were unique & engaging. It was so fun to see what Izzy & Vivvy were going to do next, all at the same time discovering the best & not so best about humanity. The end will leave you cheering!" – **RS**

"I really enjoyed reading this, and it's definitely one that will make you think. The fantasy elements allow you to take a new look at different issues and the way people behave, and I think there are some great messages in this. I really liked getting to know the characters of Izzy and Vivvy and all the other people involved in their lives – a very interesting and enjoyable read."
–Anonymous

To my beloved husband.

Acknowledgements

First of all, I would like to thank my dear husband for his constant emotional support. He also read the manuscript several times and contributed some very original and helpful ideas on how to change it.

Secondly, I would like to thank my parents, my brother, his wife, and my husband's parents and sisters for having faith in me. The same goes for all my friends.

Last but not least, I would like to thank all my creative writing teachers from primary school to university.

Disclaimer:

1. This is a work of fiction. Names, characters, places and incidents are the products of the author's imagination or are used fictitiously. Any resemblance to actual events, business establishments, locales, or persons, living or dead, is entirely coincidental.
2. This novel is appropriate for persons age 15 and above.

Chapter

1

Coming out of a misty valley, I strove to find a path among thousand-year-old oaks and young ferns ready to unfold. As thick as the mist might have been, making me crash into the lower branches – it was thin in comparison to the fog in my head.

I had spent three years trying to adjust to the city life of Skyscraper City. At first I had just tried to "jump in and swim". I rented a flat in one of the busiest street and stuffed earplugs in my ears every evening in an attempt to cope with the noise. Yet the pressure of the earplugs gradually made my head hurt. So, I decided to use another approach. Having no earplugs in my ears, the noise was so intense I naturally could not fall into a decent slumber. Thus I imagined that the noise from the traffic was actually the sound of a wide but rapid river. This natural image of a majestic flow of water sufficiently calmed my nerves to enable me to fall asleep.

And sleep I had to, for I had a serious job to go to in the morning. I had joined a circus. Being a dwarf, I was sought after, but to my chagrin at first they did not really know how to put me to use. Consequently, the first few months were really boring. I would sit around the whole day, feeling completely useless. I invented a number of mental games to keep myself busy while I was waiting and hoping they would find some work for me.

One of my most interesting approaches to killing time was also full of vanity. I would imagine I was an acrobat. I would sit in the big tent and observe the professional acrobats rehearsing. Then, after a while, I would close my eyes and imagine I was one of them. Suddenly, a feeling of elegance utterly irresistible entered my whole body and the feelings of inadequacy of being a dwarf amongst humans vanished. I would twirl in the air like a happy sparrow, do somersaults like a dolphin and sometimes fall like a bag of cement. It was fun!

Once I was so immersed in my daydreaming that my boss had to tap me on my shoulder five times before I realized I was wanted. Happy to have finally been wanted, I opened my eyes wide and smiled the smile of a devoted servant. The errand was short and easy to perform, but most amusing.

"Please take this parcel back to the nearest post office. It is addressed to a certain Mrs. Curcuis. The postman must have been in a hurry and thought it said circus. Since we are the only circus in town, he brought it here. Also: the name of the street is impossible to read. Hence the mistake."

I smiled the sweetest smile and answered: "I would be glad to sort this out."

The boss glared at me in doubt. He wrinkled his forehead, peered in very close, and made me feel really little. After an extended silence he finally seemed to have found the right words:

"You are new in town. Do you even know where the post office is?"

I was so full of confidence in myself that I surprised myself:

"Oh, don't worry. I'll find it."

He wrinkled his forehead so intensely that I feared he would squeeze his eyeballs out. Once again there was this frightful silence, followed by another array of short sentences. My boss was not the talkative type:

"Go to the office of our secretary, Miss Catherine. She'll explain where the post office is."

I spoke my last words while moving towards Miss Catherine's office, for I no longer wished to be exposed to the dreadful expression on my boss's face:

"I'll go see her right now."

I ran off so quickly that I almost dropped the parcel. The boss shook his head in disbelief and let me go without adding anything.

Upon entering Miss Catherine's office I was pleasantly surprised to finally find a smiling face. A true panacea after the frightful facial expressions of my boss I'd had to deal with seconds earlier.

She uttered in a voice as soft as angel:

"H-h-how may I h-h-help you?"

I tried not to react to her stammer in order not to insult her in any way. A lump formed in my throat, so it took me a while to loosen up and ask her:

"The boss asked me to take this parcel back to the post office. You see, it's been delivered here by mistake. But I'm new in town. Could you please tell me where the nearest post office is?"

She spoke with concern:

"Oh, it is q-q-quite far away. H-h-half an hour's w-w-walk from here. But I c-c-can drive you in my c-c-car, if you wish. I have to run some e-e-errands downtown and the p-p-post office is on my way. I'm sure you can m-m-manage the way back on foot, for there will be no m-m-more burden to carry."

I almost started to jump up and down from excitement. Not so much because of the lift offered, it was more due to the fact that I would get a ride from such a sweet lady.

Overwhelmed by joy, I almost forgot to answer:

"Oh yes, that would be most excellent."

She put some folders in her handbag and we went down to the parking lot. Her white car was so small it was quite convenient to be a dwarf. She was little for a lady herself. The drive downtown must have taken about three minutes, but it felt like ten seconds it was so exciting. As much as I was glad to have been driven and not forced to carry the parcel all the way, I was also sad to leave the car and the heart-warming company of Miss Catherine.

Before long, I found myself in a totally different atmosphere, encircled by laughing customers at the post office. The laughter at the post office arose from my clumsy but persistent attempts to pronounce the surname correctly.

"This was delivered to the circus, but is actually addressed to Mrs. Sirkuuuz."

A big hahaha rumbled among the people in line behind me.

I knew that turning back would increase my embarrassment,

so I chose to focus my eyes on the clerk in front of me. I tried to pronounce the surname again and again:

"Sersuuuz … eeeh, no … Sirkwiiiz … no … Sirkeeez … oof …"

No matter how I tried to glue a French tone to it, it always came out more or less ridiculous. The clerk had already guessed what the problem was while I was still trying to adjust my throat and lips in order to get the French pronunciation out of my mouth. In the end the clerk had to speak in a soothing voice in order to calm me down:

"Listen, mister …"

Oh, how I liked being called mister. It made me feel taller.

"… I don't need you to pronounce the surname right. Frankly speaking, I don't know how to pronounce it correctly myself. But it doesn't matter. All the postman needs is the spelling. I will underline the surname and the street name in red ink. And will also write in big red letters: NOT THE CIRCUS! So now you can leave. You have done your job. Thank you for bringing the parcel back. Have a nice day!"

You see, there is this nasty trait I have: I tend to get too passionate about things at times. Having a line of customers behind me, I managed to sober up and apologize for the lengthy experimentation with the pronunciation. Being small was most helpful in a situation like that for I could literally vanish from a post office full of people tired of waiting for a dwarf to finally speak correctly.

I was so overwhelmed by my first assignment that I almost ran back to the circus while going over the incident in my mind. In the end, the boss did not want to hear my story and there I was, once again daydreaming by the central arena.

Until one day when my boss got up on the wrong side of the bed and started yelling at me:

"Hey you, Izzy! It's O.K. if you rest here on the sidelines. Especially now that I have no work for you. But it really doesn't look good if you sleeeep!!!"

With his last word he leaned down until his face was right next to mine. I could smell his bad breath. His voice was so shrill and his facial expression so furious that I shuddered with fear. Surprisingly, there was no lump in my throat this time and I managed to utter something in my defense:

"I was not sleeping sir. I was just lost in amazement. The elegance of the acrobats really takes my breath away."

Sadly, the boss did not seem to buy my story and he yelled again, perhaps this time in a lower and more silent voice, keeping his head a bit further away:

"I am paying you to be focused on the circus not to breathe hard!"

He ended the sentence abruptly and went to his office without saying goodbye.

I grew even smaller under the pressure of his shrill voice, which echoed and gradually filled the whole central arena. All the rehearsing acrobats had stopped and were looking in my direction. Some of them even pointed and laughed. I could not decide whether it was due to what the boss had just yelled at me, or because they were seeing such a tiny creature for the first time and found me funny. The pressure of this unexpected audience grew so strong that I started to move to another dimension. I was still there in the big tent, but I could not hear the beastly humans and their shapes became fuzzier. It is a special state that dwarfs enter into when being attacked. Especially those that have a lot to do with humans must learn this maneuver.

I must confess, I felt anything but brave. I felt scared, reduced to a ridiculed miniature, sorry I had entered the world of humans, stupid to think I could make a difference in a world so full of social status rules and so void of human emotion and so on and on. Nevertheless, each evening, when I connected telepathically with our eldest dwarf, I managed to find at least one little reason to plod on in this perilous labyrinth of human relations. I would usually remember a sparkle in someone's eye that opened new horizons of hope for me and my fellow dwarves.

After half a day of trudging through a foggy forest trying to find my way home, I slammed into a tree trunk so heavily I had to lie down for a while. Safely nestled on a soft bed of moss, I suddenly realized it would have been much wiser to wait there for the fog to clear. Having made the decision to wait the fog out, a process ran through my brain that could be called a movie. All the memories from my city-life period proceeded to come alive in perfect chronological order.

I remembered the day that the boss finally found some more regular work for me to do. He said in a neutral tone, for a kind tone was not part of his repertoire:

"I need a singer. Some members of the audience have complained that we haven't had any singing acts lately. Can you sing?"

I started to sing one of the old songs that we dwarfs liked to sing at our gatherings. And I proceeded with several other songs very popular among our kind. I was trying to make an impression, so I really sang out loud. Luckily, the first song started with a simple melody, thus allowing my vocal cords to warm up sufficiently so as not to break down in the middle of my act. Another happy coincidence was the fact that I was singing in the big top, where the acoustics of the arena gave my voice more power. Consequently, I also felt more confident about my singing. In the end, I was so eager I had to make myself to stop singing after having repeated the final refrain of the tenth song five times. I was so happy to have succeeded that a tear poured out of my left eye. I could not decide whether I was overjoyed with singing or with the fact that I finally had some work to do.

The boss nodded and said: "You are good to go."

The next morning I woke up whispering, for I could not speak. My vocal cords were slightly swollen from the effort I had put into my singing the day before. I could live with the pain, but I dreaded facing my boss. I tried to cure my voice with some honey and sage, but to no avail for I would also need some time to heal. In the end, I was late for work. On top of that, I had to whisper to my boss:

"Sorry boss. I have a sore throat. My voice is gone for the day."

As I had been expecting and fearing from the very minute I woke up, he started to yell at me:

"You lazy fool of a singer! I guess you'll be sweeping the whole big top!"

He turned on his heels and I thought that was it, for it was a habit of his to leave without saying good-bye, were he angry. Yet this time, he came back with an old broom one could hardly have called useful any longer. Its working days were clearly over. He handed the broom over to me and yelled his last words for the day:

"Sweep! I want the central ring shining!"

It was evidently meant as punishment, for the floor was already very clean. Sweeping for the sake of sweeping.

I forced myself to see the sweeping as exercise and not as a punishment, which made my day rather pleasant in the end. I even started humming a joyful tune towards the end of the day.

A few minutes before my working hours were over the boss came by and to my utter surprise he apologized:

"I have spoken to an expert. A professional singer told me that losing one's voice after a performance is only a sign of effort. He said I should have you sing again when you recover. You ought to be passionate about singing, so he said."

His unexpected kindness and understanding gave me enough confidence to ask him a favor:

"Could I please have a couple of days off to start slowly at home? At home I would not be so pressured to perform perfectly. Thus I could get my voice in shape in about five days, I believe."

He said: "I could live with that. You can go home now."

At home I tried to connect – telepathically – with our Wizard of Singing, but I was not successful at it. I almost gave up, on the verge of total despair, when I suddenly realized that it might be a lot easier to reconnect with a creature of the Wood of Aquarius in an actual forest. But where was I to find a forest in a big city? A gleam of hope arose when I thought of the large central park. It was not exactly a forest, but some parts were left rather alone and much resembled a semi-cared-for forest. I hopped on my feet, eager to seek advice from the wise.

I nearly ran all the way to the park and endeavored to pick the safest place in it, where I would not be disturbed. I hid myself in the bushes close to a neglected and hence largely deserted pond, left alone by everyone except the frogs. I sat on the moist ground, using my leather jacket as a cushion. I was hot from walking and thus had had to take it off anyway. The croaking frogs provided a melody that took my mind off city life and back to where I belonged: the ancient forest populated with wise dwarfs. Then I closed my eyes and I was able to see and hear the old Wizard of Singing. He seemed to know what troubled me. He told me:

"You must drink hot lemonade with three large spoonfuls of forest honey three times a day. Also, you must cook sage tea and cool it. Then gargle it first thing in the morning and before going to bed in the evening."

I nodded in gratitude and thought that would be all, but then he spoke again:

"I will tell you about singing now. The first day, that is tomorrow, you should sing very simple melodies, but not more than three times for ten minutes. The second day you have to do everything the same, except you should prolong the singing sessions from ten minutes to half an hour. The third day, you should not sing at all. I can assure you that on the fourth day your trouble will be gone."

And so it transpired, just as he had foreseen. The fifth day I was back at work and my boss was happy to hear me rehearse diligently. After a week of practicing my singing he hired a professional to assess me and I was reviewed well enough to be able to perform the next Sunday, when there was an audience there to hear me.

Having substantial confidence in the acoustics of the central ring, I still had a great deal of anxiety to deal with. I could make a list of the fears I was submerged in while performing. The feeling that I was singing out of tune was one of the worst. It grew so strong that it conned me into believing that I was actually imagining new melodies while singing. The melodies were pleasant to the ear. Thus, in a most absurd way, I actually found the thought a bit soothing at times.

No matter how disturbing the numerous fears were, there was also an advantage to them. At least I did not sing with my full voice and therefore my vocal cords survived the first performance intact.

The audience seemed to like my performance. Even though the clapping might to some extent be a habit, I was pretty sure that I could see sparks in the eyes of the listeners in the first row. And sparks are something one cannot fake. They tend to make certain moments in life a lot more memorable and they are more felt than really seen. They might be just an accompanying phenomenon to the magical bond between two beings who for a while manage to resonate at the same frequency. To resonate with another creature at the same frequency, be it for only a brief moment, might be the most magical thing in life. It is hard to describe, but it is as real as it gets.

After three weeks of disciplined rehearsal and three Sundays of satisfying singing experience, I had an epiphany while taking a stroll in the park on a free Monday. I must have been humming all the way without knowing. What I did notice was that people were staring at me. First I thought it was merely due to the fact that there were not many dwarfs in the streets of the big city. Upon thinking about it for a while, I realized that most of the people staring at me were regular visitors to the park. We had seen each other before on several occasions. So I wondered why they would be so surprised and bewildered.

I started to sing out loud in order to get my mind off the annoying stares. To my utter surprise, the stares grew longer and occasionally a jaw would drop in astonishment. It must have been upon the third dropped jaw that my epiphany took place. From the very first day in the big city to that moment had I not heard a living soul sing or even hum. What for a dwarf or any elementary being of the forest was almost like breathing was most peculiar to the humans of the big city.

When I first arrived in the new environment, I had been too

tense to sing. The habit of singing only came back to life after three successful performances in the central arena. And in the park that day I realized that I was perceived as a weird phenomenon. At first I tried to adjust to the idiosyncrasies of the city and put a lot of effort into not singing in public. I failed to do so. The more I sang in the circus, the more difficult it was to stop the urge to hum and sing as a semi-conscious habit in my spare time.

Being forced to accept my sinister habit, I gradually learned to look down while walking in public, thus avoiding the stares.

It seemed to work out just fine for a time. After a while, though, I realized that I was becoming anti-social. I would no longer greet people, nor would I say a few words with the acquaintances I had acquired. Looking to the ground and singing put me in touch with the darker corners of my mind. I became genuinely lonely and sad. Even my repertoire was increasingly comprised of sad songs.

The change in my repertoire did not bring much joy and satisfaction to either the audience or my boss. Therefore, my boss hired a delicate soul, a young beauty called Vivvy, to sing with me in a duet. She had sung in a choir as a girl and needed a job in the city.

Vivvy was not just my co-singer. We also became friends. Often after work we would go for a cup of coffee and chat. She was the first human I got to know really well. If it were just about her, I would have a lot of faith in people. She was kind, compassionate, considerate, and honest. She never made me feel I was worth less for being so small. I thought to myself:

Maybe I cannot do much to change the world of humans, but I can surely make it my mission in life to protect this fortress of goodness – my dear friend Vivvy.

Nevertheless, after a long conversation with Vivvy about singing, we thought we'd discovered a way to open the hearts of people a little. I was actually whining about not being able to sing and hum while walking in the park. It proved to be a starting point for a lengthy conversation about habits. I told Vivvy:

"Singing out loud in public is a very normal thing among dwarfs. Actually, there is no real distinction between public and private, as far as singing is concerned. When you feel like singing, you simply sing. No one will pay much attention, unless you are really loud. And in that case, others will usually join in and sing along."

Vivvy was pleasantly surprised:

"Oh, that sounds great. I wish I could see it for real some time."

Having an attentive listener, I went on bragging about the ways of dwarfs:

"Singing silently or humming for us dwarfs is a way of overcoming boredom or solitude. And singing out loud is a way of expressing emotions. If one is sad, one sings a mourning song. Being angry about something or at somebody, one sings a marching piece. While falling in love, it is obviously a love song that does the trick. When really happy, one chooses a joyful tune. Such a melody also comes in handy if one is depressed. Depression usually means that we are exhausted from work or a months-long sadness."

Vivvy added with a tinge of sadness in her beautiful brown eyes:

"Humans used to have very similar habits, but long ago they abandoned them. At some point in human history it became unfashionable to show emotions. A person that showed emotions would be regarded as childish at best and retarded or mentally ill at worst. People grew ashamed of their emotions. Therefore, they gradually learned to not show them in any way."

I was appalled:

"Not show emotions at all? That is so unhealthy!"

Vivvy continued:

"If there are tears, they would have to be hidden. If somebody is laughing out of sheer joy, no joke involved, others will ask him whether he has been drinking. The only state when emotions are allowed is the state of being drunk, because one can always blame it on the alcohol. And if it's the drink, it isn't really you. And just like any other way of expressing emotions, also singing in public was abandoned, except under the influence of liquor, of course."

I could not help myself but to add some of the wisdom I had learned back in the Wood of Aquarius:

"If human beings hide emotions, it does not mean that they do not feel them. Hiding enormous quantities of emotional energy creates additional stress in human life. Playing cool at all times has its price. No wonder there are so many health problems these days. Some of them might easily come from suppressed emotions."

Vivvy nodded in agreement and looked at me as if she would like to hear some more. So I went on:

"Like anger and sadness, also love and compassion are suppressed. This leads to a society where the cruelest people seem to be the fittest to survive."

Vivvy fixed her stare at the cup she was holding in her hands and remained silent for a while. Then, all of a sudden, she almost spilled her coffee when she exclaimed:

"We could sing together!"

I did not comprehend her at first, for I thought she meant me and her and we were already singing together. But no! She was proposing something else:

"We could encourage the audience to sing along! And not just the chorus! We could hand out the lyrics and sing whole songs together."

I was enthusiastic about it too:

"What an idea!"

And so Vivvy and I went about making our dream happen. We prepared two songs that we thought would not be too difficult and towards the end of our act we handed out the lyrics to the audience. Then they simply sang along. Some individuals got so carried away that they started singing with their full voice and one could hear their distinct sound. I could hear somebody in the first row sing out of tune, but other than that, as a group they were very good.

We were in our second month of activating the audience in such a manner when, after the collective performance, a middle-aged lady approached us. She was on the verge of tears when she expressed her gratitude for the opportunity to sing. She said:

"I had liked to sing as a girl. Later I thought it was childish and I even stopped singing in the shower. I was not able to get my neighbors in the apartment building out of my mind. Whenever I started to sing, I feared I would bother the neighbors. Gradually I grew out of the habit of singing entirely."

I tried to express as much compassion as possible:

"O, that's too bad."

She added:

"It had not been until that moment in the circus that I realized how much I had given up for the sake of being serious and sane."

Vivvy smiled at the lady and leaned her head to the side, full of understanding:

"But here in the circus nobody is serious and fully sane. And you can get a little nuts every Sunday, if you wish. It's a safe place to sing."

The lady smiled back and said:

"Oh, yes, I know. That's why I have been coming here on a regular basis. And I intend to continue. Thank you for the opportunity. I am immensely grateful!"

On another occasion a young man approached and told us another amazing story:

"The singing at the circus on Sundays has inspired me to call up my old singing buddies from my college years and form a choir again. We meet on Thursdays at my place and since my house is half a mile away from any inhabited area we can sing our lungs out."

Vivvy said:

"Well, isn't that amazing!"

He also shared with us the following:

"The singing actually renewed our friendship, which had not died but had just been asleep. We had all found our careers so important that we had not dared to devote any time to old friends."

I could not help but moralize:

"That is so typical in the human world. You strive to be successful and at the end of the day there is nobody to share your success with."

The man went on:

"Oh, yes, I realized that, when I got promoted. And then I saw a poster announcing the new singing act at the circus on Sundays. I felt the solution was somehow connected to singing. So I came to your circus. Thank you for giving us the opportunity to sing."

After a few months of singing together, a couple approached and told us their story. First, the lady let her man do the talking:

"We both used to sing as youngsters in a choir. That is also how we first met. Later, we both abandoned the habit of singing due to more serious engagements. We met again at a business event and fell in love. We married soon for we already knew each other well from our teenage years. At first, none of us felt that we should sing again. In time, we became like machines. We were only performing our duties at work and at home. We became hollow inside, we stopped feeling any emotion. So also our relationship started to fall apart."

Then the man felt he should let his wife get in a word:

"Right, honey? Am I making my point?"

She took it from there:

"We tried many things to save our marriage. But none of them seemed to help as much as the singing. Which should come as no surprise. We are singers by nature! Songs are our way of expressing ourselves. We would listen to music a lot, but never sang along. We were afraid it would sound childish. It was our Sunday experiment that made us realize that there is no substitute for the actual singing!"

Having received such wonderful feedback from the audience, Vivvy and I continued to hand out the lyrics and encourage the audience to sing along. I finally felt that I was doing something worthwhile. The boss thought it was odd to make the audience sing, for they had paid to listen. However, in general he was satisfied, for there was never an empty seat on Sundays, which ensured him the cash flow he needed to run a circus.

Of course, there were also unpleasant incidents. One of the most aggravating reactions from the audience concerned an angry husband. He did not even participate in our singing session. He waited outside and came to me right after the show. He was bristling with rage. He started to yell at me without saying hello first. His sentences were incomplete, full of cursing and flavored with spittle. I only managed to grasp that he was talking about his wife, who had obviously been attending our show for a while. I had to ask him some explicit questions in order to finally find out what the problem was.

Apparently his wife had been changing due to the singing sessions. She had become happier, more confident, less dependent on her husband. She had even received a promotion at work and earned enough money to become financially independent from her husband. The husband blamed us for having ruined his marriage.

The accusation came as a shock. I was perplexed, because this was clearly not my intention. I tried to help make human relations better, not worse. That night I had trouble falling asleep, so I asked for a dream that would give me an answer to this annoying dilemma.

And on that very same night I had a vivid dream, which is a sign that dreams are trying to tell us something important regarding our lives. The dream was as follows:

I found myself in a house, where everything seemed to be

broken or out of order. The house belonged to that angry husband from the circus earlier that day. He dragged me from room to room and with great tenacity showed me everything that was wrong with the house: broken windows, electric appliances out of order, dripping taps, cold radiators, creaking doors. Whenever he showed me some damage or something broken, he explicitly blamed it on me. Yet in the dream I had a terribly strong feeling that I had absolutely nothing to do with anything that was wrong in the house.

That was the dream. I remembered from the days when I had still lived with the dwarfs of the Wood of Aquarius that the old Wizard of Dreams always interpreted a house as one's life. Thus the house in my dream would be the life of that angry husband. There were many things in his life that had gone wrong, but the strong feeling that I had nothing to do with it showed me that the singing was not the problem. The singing was an opportunity for the lady to free herself from a suffocating relationship with a hostile man.

When I woke up in the morning and interpreted the dream, I was filled with a warm feeling that I was actually helping the lady do something that she would never have accomplished on her own.

After that, I forgot about the incident, but about a month later the same lady came to me after the show and told me that our show had actually helped her to break free from a suffocating relationship and to get a divorce from a man that had been verbally hostile to her and used to put her down on every occasion. She shared with me that she was very happy to be single and felt as light as a bird, having gotten rid of the burden of an extremely controlling husband.

That day I learned two things. Firstly, I came to the conclusion that singing was always therapeutic, even when at first it might seem harmful. Secondly, I started to trust the messages in dreams.

Chapter

2

All these recollections of my life in Skyscraper City were suddenly interrupted by a fellow dwarf, who patted me on my shoulder and made me open my eyes while lying in the misty forest on my way to the Wood of Aquarius.

"Hi, Izzy! Good to see you!"

"Good to see you Herbert! How are you?"

"Oh, you know me. Running errands for wizards as usual."

"What are you doing here anyway? Who sent you? We are far from the Wood of Aquarius!"

"The old Wizard of Dreams has a telepathic connection with you. He saw you trapped by fog. So he sent me to get you."

"But how do you find your way in such thick fog?"

"Oh, that is an old art. Only few dwarfs know it. I learned it from my father. You train your eyes to see in fog."

"How wonderful!"

"Anyway, I am supposed to bring you home. The Wizard said you have been through a lot and you need to recuperate back home before you can carry on with your enthusiasm for the world of people."

"Well, thank you for coming to get me. I will gladly follow you. I am sick of this fog and weary from the whole journey. And the memories of the big city hang heavy over me."

"Follow me then."

"Please show me the way."

Herbert had to concentrate on his method of walking in thick fog, so we walked in silence. And the recollections from the city went on in my head just like a movie.

The next thing I recalled was an incident with the circus secretary, Miss Catherine. The boss was not very keen on our sing-along experiment, so he never talked about it. Catherine learned about it through a friend who had become a fan of our Sunday singing sessions. The friend sounded so excited that Catherine decided to give it a try and joined us on a sunny Sunday afternoon. I noticed her in the first row and waved at her briefly in order not to draw too much attention to her. She smiled back at me.

I thought I could hear her singing along already during the performance of our duet. She must have known most of the lyrics by heart. She tried to keep her voice down in order not to disturb our duet, but one could see that she was so passionate about singing that she could not be entirely quiet either.

Vivvy had proposed some time ago to let the audience sing along a little longer. So by the time Catherine joined us we were handing out the lyrics to five songs instead of just two. I noticed a sparkle in Miss Catherine's eyes when she accepted the sheets of paper. And then I heard her sing with her full voice. I wasn't sure what amazed me more: the fact that she didn't stammer while singing or the beauty of her silken voice.

For the third song she even stood up. She did it automatically and didn't notice it at first. When she did become aware of the fact that she'd stood up, she started to lower her body and was groping with her delicate hand to find her seat. At that very instant four other people stood up and she decided to stay up. Pretty soon everyone was up and singing like a choir. It actually became a habit to stand up while singing in the shows that followed.

Miss Catherine became one of our regular guests on Sundays, which was the only day for the audience to sing along. On all other days, that is, from Wednesday to Saturday, for the circus was closed on Mondays and Tuesdays, it would be just Vivvy and me performing. In the morning we would always rehearse and prepare for the afternoon and evening shows.

One fine morning, on my way to a smaller tent, where Vivvy and I rehearsed every workday, I bumped into Catherine. She spoke very enthusiastically about the previous Sunday:

"I absolutely adore your Sunday shows. They're f-f-fabulous! The way the audience sings along! I am really glad you two came up with the idea and w-w-went through with it despite the silent disapproval of our boss."

Anyone would have noticed that she was stammering less than usual. I was not sure what to ascribe this change to. Was it just the fact that we had become closer friends through singing? Or was it something else? I could not ask her directly. As if she had been reading my mind, she explained:

"I used to have this anti-stammering therapy, when I was a little girl. One of the things we did was to sing songs. We also used to sing our sentences in regular conversations. I only remembered that yesterday. You know, it's possible that the singing sessions on Sundays are helping me, because I noticed that I stammer m-m-much less these days."

I was so afraid of saying something wrong that I got a lump in my throat and the only response she got from me was a smile. She smiled back and went off to her work.

I could not decide whether it was sheer coincidence or not, but I started running into Catherine more and more often. Most of the time she would only smile at me. But when she did say something, her stammer was less and less obvious. Often she would tell me that she sang at home and she always included all the new songs in her repertoire. It must have been the singing that had helped her speech then.

I was so amazed by the power of singing that I once spoke to my boss about it:

"It is just an idea, so please do not get upset."

"Go on, spit it out. I haven't got all day."

"Have you noticed that Miss Catherine stammers a lot less?"

"Yes, she happens to be eventually growing out of it. Time to grow up, I say."

"Oh, she has been a grown-up for a long time now. That is not the point! She joined our singing sessions on Sundays. She said herself that the singing is helping her!"

"Oh, come on! Who would believe a silly theory like that! The next thing you dreamer are going to try to convince me about is that I should let her sing with you two in a trio!" He rolled his eyes in scorn.

"I was not going to ask you to let her perform with us. For I know that she is a good secretary and you would not like to lose her to a singing career."

He rolled his eyes in contempt again and asked restlessly:

"So what DID you have in mind then?"

"Maybe you could let her rehearse with us once a week. Less stammer …"

He interrupted me with his hand, showing me who the boss around here was:

"Listen, you tiny creature, I know what's best for her. To concentrate on her work! And not to waltz into your rehearsing tent whenever she pleases!"

I resumed: "Less stammer would make her a better secretary. I am sure you would be happy about that. And she could join us on Fridays, when she has less work to do in her office anyway."

The boss's face turned red in anger and he shouted out so loud that I had to cover my ears: "The answer is no, no, and one more time no. I'm not going to discuss this any further. As long as I'm the boss around here, she will sit at her desk and not yodel her precious and well-paid hours away! Understood?"

He dashed off, furious as hell. And I looked down in despair. I was only trying to help. He could have said no in a nice way. There was no need to shout.

I stood there in the hallway, feeling sorry for myself, so immersed in thought that I did not move. Staring at the ground I suddenly saw a hand wave in front of my eyes. I looked up and saw Catherine smiling and asking kindly:

"What's w-w-wrong Izzy?"

"Oh, it's nothing really."

"I don't believe you. Something is b-b-bothering you. Come on, you can tell me."

"I'm not sure it would be right to talk to you about it."

"Oh, it's about me! Then you ab-b-bsolutely have to tell me!"

Her eyes were piercing right through me. My self-defense broke down. I could not resist her pleading smile any longer, so I told her what had just happened.

She sighed, looked down for a second, but returned with her smile that seemed impervious to any misfortune in life:

"Oh, you don't have to worry about that! Give me some time. I'll f-f-figure something out."

And she did. By Friday the same week. She came into our rehearsal tent ten minutes late and all shining with joy, carrying some files. She explained:

"I have come to r-r-rehearse with you. In case the boss comes in, though, I will pretend that I am as-s-skiing you some questions about calculating your salary. I have p-p-prepared some questions, so that it would look genuine. O.K.?"

Vivvy and I had to smile, for we found her cute, but there was not much approval in our smiles. We did not want her to take any risks. The boss was very strict.

Vivvy tried to make sure Catherine was aware of the potential danger in this situation:

"I am not sure this is a good idea. Our boss is not a fool. He will figure it out."

Catherine was stubborn:

"Oh, no, he won't. I know how to act. I used to be a member of a special drama group. Besides, I am doing this for him. He is often embarrassed in front of clients b-b-because of my s-s-stammer."

We both looked at her and could not say anything, for we could not kill her dream. We both hoped it would turn out all right and we started rehearsing.

She would only rehearse with us for an hour on Fridays and in the afternoon she usually worked an hour longer. Thus she was not doing anything wrong. But we all knew that if the boss found out, he wouldn't be very happy. Still, we enjoyed rehearsing together and we tried to put our fears behind us.

Catherine was improving as a singer and one could also notice that her stammer had lessened. One Friday morning she came in to rehearse and was glowing with joy. She said:

"Do you know what the boss said to me yesterday just before I finished working in the office?"

Vivvy and I asked with some trepidation in our voices: "What?"

"He said that my stammer had improved!"

"Oh, that is good news!"

"Do you think I should tell him about our rehearsing?"

We tried to persuade her to keep it a secret, for the boss had already expressed his opinion on the topic. He simply did not believe it could help. He was probably ascribing the improvement to pure chance. Yet Catherine could not keep the secret anymore. One day she told the boss about the Friday rehearsals. Just as Vivvy and I had feared, he burst out in anger:

"What? You have been singing during working hours? You are lucky it has only been an hour a week. Otherwise I would fire you! How long has this ridiculous thing been going on?"

Catherine struggled to get the two words out of her mouth: "T-t-two m-m-months."

The boss was strict as usual: "Listen. I will reduce your next pay by eight hours. And I don't want you to sing anymore. Understood? Or else I will fire you!"

She wanted to tell him that she had worked an hour longer on Fridays, but the lump in her throat was so big and the fear of a tremendous stammer was so strong that she did not manage to say anything.

Catherine soon told us about the shouting and she never spoke about it again. She went back to her usual stammer. She would still join us occasionally on Sundays, but she never sang with a full voice again. The boss had demolished her dream.

I struggled with this for a long time. However, in the end I had to realize that no matter how sincere and devoted I might be, I could never help everyone.

I even had a reassuring dream shortly after Catherine stopped rehearsing with us:

I was riding around the countryside with Catherine at the wheel. In real life, I was not a driver, but in the dream I surprisingly knew how to drive a car. I noticed that Catherine had problems shifting gears. Initially I was too polite to say anything, yet later it started to get on my nerves. All of a sudden I exclaimed:

"Oh, Catherine! You cannot shift gears like that! You have to do it smoothly. There is too much noise coming from the engine, every time you shift!"

"But how am I supposed to do it? This is the only way I know how!" She looked at me desperately and stopped the car.

"Let's change seats. I'll show you."

So I drove around and shifted gears as often as possible for about half an hour. Then we changed seats again. Catherine had not learned a thing. On the contrary, her shifting had gotten worse.

That was the dream. It was very vivid and I remembered it very well in the morning. Thus, it must have had a hidden message. A car usually means one's job or business. It was Catherine's car, so it must have meant her job as a secretary. In the dream I was interfering with it. I was trying to teach her how to do her job. The old Wizard of Dreams said that in dreams we should always drive our car and not let others drive it for us. It had been wrong of me to drive Catherine's car. I had to let her drive it her way. Which in real life meant that I should let her stammer. I should leave her alone and stop trying to help her. At the end of the dream there was a very significant feeling overwhelming me: the feeling that her way of driving the car was acceptable and didn't need to be improved.

So there I was: putting joy in the lives of those that dared to sing along on Sundays. It became a routine. And falling into a routine always gives me the feeling that I can do more. I developed this mind-boggling obsession to find something else to analyze and improve. I had been like that since childhood. The wizards of our dwarf community that took care of schooling young dwarfs had to give me additional homework to keep my mind occupied. Otherwise I would have gone out and explored the dangers of the Wood of Aquarius myself. They also taught me many meditative techniques that calmed my mind to some extent. Despite all their efforts, there was a little flame burning in my mind that could be called genuine curiosity. No meditative technique was able to make it just smolder, let alone die out.

Even age and experience seemed to have had little influence over that flame of curiosity when I found Vivvy's notebook on the floor. Even the sense of decency had left me and I read through it like one would read through a mystery novel full of suspense. Later I gave it to Vivvy, of course without saying a word about having read it.

I was ashamed of what I had done and I wanted to forget about it. Nevertheless the appointments from Vivvy's notebook kept swirling around in my memory and made me restless. There was one particular detail that bothered me. Apart from doctor appointments and errands like buying something specific, there were only female names jotted down. Was Vivvy single? The girl was in her early thirties and I thought she should have been dating.

Vivvy caught me lost in my thoughts repeatedly. One day she posed a direct question:

"What has been occupying your mind so intensely lately?"

"Nothing."

"You are lying!"

"Sorry."

"Go on! Tell me!"

"Well … I am really ashamed to admit it. Do you remember the other day when I found your appointment notebook?"

"Don't tell me. I know. You read through it."

"How do you know?"

"How else would you know that it contains appointments? It does not say anything on the cover."

"Sorry."

"It's no big deal. But why are you so worried about it?"

"Well … eh … it seems like you are still single."

"And? It's fashionable to be single these days."

"Really? The human world has really changed a lot."

And then she changed the topic for she obviously was not prepared to discuss this sensitive subject.

Nevertheless, I kept pondering the fact that a young girl like Vivvy would not only be single but also completely comfortable with it.

And then one sunny Sunday I noticed that a young man in the front row kept staring at Vivvy. A gleam of hope arose in me, but I did not say or do anything in order to not spoil the occasion. He acted the same way the following Sunday and the Sunday after that ... After a month Vivvy finally noticed him. She was furious:

"Did you see the guy in the front row? He kept staring at me! What is wrong with him?"

"Wrong? That's new to me. I thought in the human world it was normal to like a girl if you are a boy."

"But I don't need a boy! I am perfectly happy being single!"

"Well ... what do you want me to do? Put up a sign at the entrance saying: Young guys not allowed?"

"Don't be silly. It just bothers me, that's all."

I refused to add anything and smiled contently. I thought to myself: whatever was bound to happen was going to happen. And it did. At the end of the second month of periodical staring from the first row, the young man approached Vivvy after our communal singing session. I stepped aside, but observed them from a distance. I saw Vivvy blush, which must have been a good sign, for I had never seen her blush before. She was looking down and smiled meekly. He kept talking, but she would not lift her face and look at him. In the end, he dared to take her by the hand and she finally looked up and nodded. I'd guessed right that they had a date. I was so happy I almost started jumping up and down, but instead I went to the dressing room and never said a thing.

Luckily it was Vivvy who started to talk about it. It must have been shortly after their first date. She said:

"You know the guy in the front row I was complaining about?"

"Yes. What about him?" I was trying to act like I was not thinking about him and her just about every day since I'd first noticed him staring at Vivvy.

"Well, he asked me out and we went on a date together." Her beautiful brown eyes were glinting like pearls, gently surrounded by her abundant brown hair.

"And?"

"Well I don't know what to do! On one hand, I like my freedom being single. But on the other hand, I think I'm in love. He's my first thought when I wake up in the morning and my last thought before I fall asleep in the evening. When I see him or hear his voice on the phone, I get butterflies in my stomach. What do you think I should do?"

I knew exactly what she should do, but I did not want to spoil the moment by being too direct. So I tried to be diplomatic and said:

"Whenever we find ourselves in a dilemma, we dwarfs ask for an answer in our dreams. Perhaps you could try it as well."

"Oh, what a great idea. I will try it this evening!"

The next morning she came to work more perplexed than ever. She described her dream to me with a great deal of concern in her voice:

"In my dream, I was taking a walk by a beautiful river with a woman that does not exist in real life. We were good friends. I felt very close to her. First we were walking in silence and marveling at the swift crystal-clear river, the fish swimming in it and the birds flying over the stream as if they were trying to catch some of its freshness. There were also some ducks swimming against the current for a while and then turning to go with the flow. It was springtime and most trees were in blossom. The scent of flower nectar filled the air and lifted our spirits. All of a sudden, the woman smiled at me and took my hand as if it were the most natural thing to do. She told me how much she enjoyed my company and how much our friendship meant to her. My heart filled with love and I kissed her.

At that point I woke up because I was horrified. Knowing I was not a lesbian, the kiss really froze the blood in my veins. What was that supposed to mean?"

I giggled at the common mistake people make when interpreting dreams of an erotic nature. Then I reassured her:

"The woman in your dream represents the female aspect of your personality. The dream is telling you to become more connected with that aspect. Simply put: you should be more feminine."

"More feminine? But how does this answer my question about the guy I am seeing?"

"The dream is telling you that you have become too comfortable being single. You have developed the attitude that you do not need anyone, particularly not a man. Being feminine also entails this part of being in a love relationship, being less than perfect, a bit fragile, in a dialogue with men."

"So, basically, the answer to my dilemma is a big affirmative as regards continuing to date this guy?"

"Precisely."

"Oof, that comes as a surprise! I was hoping the dream would tell me to dump him. I was really set in my ways being single."

"It is always wise to listen to the messages in dreams, the old wizards used to say."

"Well, I guess my dreams have left me no choice but to keep dating him. I hope it turns out to be a good relationship."

"The dream does not guarantee you that it will be a good one. But it is the bad relationships that in the end guide us to the good ones that we are meant for. No pain no gain."

"I had a relationship in my early twenties. My heart ended up being broken. That day I swore to myself I would never let any other guy hurt me. I decided to stay single till the day I die. Yet somehow I fell in love with this guy and it seems like there is no way back now."

"Life goes on, not back. A scar in your heart only means an additional experience. It should not determine your actions until the day you die."

"I guess you're right. Besides, I really like the guy. I probably couldn't stop dating him even if I wanted to."

"Enjoy being young and don't worry now."

Vivvy soon forgot about her promise to herself to stay single for life, for she was having a really good time with Christopher. He turned out to be an exquisite dancer. They used every opportunity to go out dancing.

Chapter

3

Vivvy and Christopher had the time of their lives. Vivvy had been dancing for as long as she could remember, but rarely in a pair. She preferred to dance alone in her room. She would put on some passionate dance music and dance like a wild beast in the privacy of her home. If no one could see her, she would flow with the music and forget about everything. Those were the moments when she could really be herself. No judgment from herself or others. No audience to please. No roles, no games, just dancing.

She could still remember the school dances where she had tried to dance with a number of boys. It had never worked. She would automatically start leading and step on the poor guy's feet time in time. She eventually gave up, for she felt really sorry for the guys.

Everything changed when she met Christopher, though. Being an experienced and extremely talented dancer, he would grab her firmly and twirl her across the dance floor so quickly she couldn't think and thus could not lead.

When I first saw them dance, I was overwhelmed. They seemed to be made for each other. Vivvy invited me and Miss Catherine to join them. We tried to dance ourselves, but most of the time we preferred to sit behind a table with a good view of the dance floor; we sat back comfortably and just watched this fabulous couple dance their feet sore from the enthusiasm they brought to waltzing.

Despite our happy faces glinting from behind the table, Vivvy and Chris wouldn't stop trying to persuade Cathy and me to dance. They turned out to be good teachers and in a few months we managed to learn to waltz, tango, and cha-cha-cha quite decently for such an odd couple as ourselves: a dwarf and a tiny lady. Well, we might have been tiny, but full of passion.

***

Something interrupted my recollections of the dancing period in Skyscraper City. It was a large boulder, seemingly unconquerable at first. While surmounting it following Herbert in that fog, I remembered a funny incident that had happened while learning to waltz.

***

I was just getting the hang of it, when I suddenly felt that we were swirling too fast. I got scared. I asked in a panic:

"How do you stop this?"

Cathy stopped dancing and grabbed her belly, for she was in physical pain from laughing so hard. At first I was perplexed, but then I started to laugh myself, for the whole scene was almost beyond ridiculous.

Unable to dance, Cathy and I went back to our table and sat down. Upon catching our breath after giggling like little kids, Vivvy and Chris approached with concern. They had seen the incident from afar and had come to check up on us.

Cathy explained what had happened and Vivvy had to keep her sides from splitting too. Chris was a moderate giggler, so he did not exactly need to restrain himself, yet he still had a good laugh. How do you stop the left turns while waltzing? Either you change to right turns or you sway. It was the Vienna waltz

- 46 -

of course, the English waltz is slower.

Having fun? Human beings rarely manage to have fun without getting drunk first. They worry too intensely. Well, I must say that this period of dancing was to a substantial degree carefree. The music took us far from the worries and intrigues one has to put up with in the world of men and women.

The circus was closed Mondays and Tuesdays, so we danced on our two free evenings. We would go to a downtown dance club called The Swirling Swingers. And if we were really enthusiastic about a new dance step, or just wanted to jump and waltz, we would meet even more often.

Some moments at The Swirling Swingers were hilarious, some were poignant, yet they all filled our hearts with laughter and joy. We would jive and hop, hug and spin like a roulette. Chris taught us the basics of standard and Latin American dances and then he let us express ourselves. After a few months of teaching, he stopped interfering and correcting us, for he felt we had no need to become professional dancers.

Sometimes we were too tired to dance. We met anyway, sat behind our table and watched other couples dance. Our eyes were glinting with admiration. Some couples were so great at various choreographed moves that we had to show our adulation by briefly applauding.

Naturally there were also gloomy days, like full moon days, for instance. We would sit behind table number seven, and grunt and rant about everything, criticizing the dancing couples, and we never even had the decency to get up and dance a song or two. Having sat out all the songs, we left with our faces like lemons. But that was only due to the full moon, thus we paid no special attention to such dreary occasions.

There was a slightly sore incident that really stuck in my mind. I smelled trouble when she entered the club. I was observing her from our table. The first thing she did upon stepping through the front door was to thrust her jacket and over-coat into the hands of her male companion, as if he were her own personal slave.

Having freed herself from the burden of her exquisite fashion style, she yelled at the receptionist for no apparent reason. Wearing the latest designer red dancing shoes with heels higher than the foothills of the Himalayas, she later stepped onto the dance floor and almost collapsed from being so clumsy. And then she yelled at her dance partner. Again for no apparent reason.

I forgot about her while swirling with my dear friend Cathy passionately, when all of a sudden all I could hear was a cry. A cry so shrill it pierced right through my ears. It struck like lightning catching a hiker by surprise, all alone up in the mountains immersed in thought about the marshes of human emotion, down in the valley of man and woman.

I turned back and saw the high-heeled lady bend over, grabbing her toes and screaming from the alleged pain. Then she straightened up and gave me a look. A look that could kill the toughest dwarf in the universe, were he not wise enough to look away. I looked away, which made her even angrier, of course. Consequently she started yelling at me:

"You impertinent midget! You stepped on my toes! It hurts!"

I'd had enough of her arrogance and verbal abuse and I yelled back:

"The way you are yelling here like a mad cow, my ears hurt! And I am not the only one you are causing pain to!"

The music stopped and the deejay came down from his studio to clarify the situation. The security guy was out sick, thus the deejay had to do his job too. Once faced with a higher authority, the touchy lady started to imagine things:

"He's trying to kill me!"

The deejay tried to remain calm: "What did he do?"

I decided to wait to hear her false accusations. She had a very vivid imagination:

"He did it on purpose! I saw him staring at me. He hates me because I am taller than him. He did it on purpose! He stepped on my toes. Look, they are swelling!"

The deejay obviously knew how to handle women. Looking for a victim was not his cup of tea. He knew well enough that little accidents often happen on the dance floor, especially on a crowded night like that one.

Being a wise and experienced dance floor manager, he took her upstairs and had a chat with her. In the meantime, he turned the music back on. I could not help myself from looking upstairs into his studio, which was closed up front with transparent glass. She kept talking and he was a patient listener. By the time she got back on the dance floor she must have forgotten all about the incident, for she smiled at me.

Obviously she had just needed a shoulder to cry on. Ah, women!

Subsequently, the four of us ended up giggling at the table again, replaying the incident in our conversation over and over again. We let our imaginations go wild and had a great time again. In the end, the incident turned out to not be as troublesome as initially expected.

Time was passing. We were getting along well together, gyrating our bodies in the waves of the music and our minds in the flow of our humorous imagination. Those were the months of having good old-fashioned fun. Of course, we had a care or two, but they never really got serious, for the good mood prevailed.

Perhaps I should mention the story with an old alcoholic. The more he swirled, the thirstier he became. Instead of drinking water or juice, he drank wine. He lost all sense of self-criticism due to the large quantities of alcohol in his blood, so he kept swirling and drinking.

His wife was very patient. One could notice that she had been putting up with his drinking for years. There was no sparkle in her eyes. The gloominess of her stare showed apathy and perpetual oblivion.

She did not even try to persuade him to stop this dancing-and-drinking nonsense and go home. Two or three times she even saved him from falling. A brave and strong woman she was.

There came a moment, though, it was around midnight, when she could not save him from falling. He dropped like a sack of potatoes and lost consciousness. She did not panic. Far from it. Her eyes did not even twinkle. For her, it must have been pure routine to call an ambulance. Other people approached and the deejay checked his breathing and pulse, while she just stood there and waited for the ambulance.

The alcoholic was breathing and his heart was alright. He had just lost consciousness due to his high blood-alcohol level. She must have known. Thus, she did not stir. After the EMTs had carried his unconscious body to the ambulance, she fainted herself. I barely managed to catch her and prevent her from falling. I tried to signal the people around me to stop the ambulance, but nobody paid attention for their eyes were focused on the vehicle leaving the parking lot in front of the dance club. I dragged her to a chair, and once seated, she quickly regained consciousness.

She could not stop saying thank you for what I had done. We got involved in a lengthy conversation. I learned a lot of painful details about their story:

"This whole thing might seem totally stupid to you, but it is his only outlet. He prefers getting drunk once a month to being on tranquillizers. And I must say, I don't blame him. I tried to take a pill they prescribed for him. The side effects were awful. You must think we are total jerks."

"On the contrary! Spill your guts. I'm a good listener."

"Oof, you are a life saver. Well, there is more to the story. My husband did not simply start drinking out of boredom. His parents are around seventy, but his mother still puts up with his father. He is an aggressive alcoholic and she takes his blows as if it were some kind of routine. There are a million things she could do and my husband is more than willing to help her. That's what drives him crazy. He has been watching his mum being beaten his entire life. The old creep is so cunning – he never causes her any serious injury. Thus the police and the social services can't do a thing."

"Not a thing?!"

"Well, my husband could press charges, if his mother were willing to testify."

"And she won't?!"

"No. You see, she goes to church every Sunday and the priest always tells her that marriage is for life and that she should love him even more, because enough love can cure anything. That sort of crap, you know."

"Horrible."

"Well, I guess if we provide the paramedics and doctors with some work, there's not much harm in that. What do you think?"

"Oh, don't worry about the strong guys that have just taken your husband away. They need exercise." I giggled and saw her giggle for the first time.

"Thank you. You are so considerate and understanding," she said and squeezed my hand in gratitude.

A seemingly dramatic incident ended well anyhow. There were funny incidents too.

Like, for example, the time that Vivvy forgot her skirt at home. She was wearing a long silk blouse that reached just over her hips. She was so distracted that she had forgotten to put on her skirt. Chris must have been distracted too, thus they noticed her lack of a decent skirt when she entered the dance club. When I saw her I burst out laughing, but the very next minute I was persuading her that she looked just fine. Since miniskirts had a funny tendency to get shorter and shorter, her blouse could be perceived as a tunic.

It proved difficult to convince her, so we kept laughing around the table and Chris kept pouring wine, for he had no intention of driving back just because her sexy bottom might show while dancing. The black underwear looked decent anyway.

Just when the evening was turning into a chatting fest, no dancing involved, Vivvy was apparently so drunk that she forgot about her dilemma and dragged Chris onto the dance floor. They danced like crazy. And the crowd was watching. I am sure no one suspected that she was missing her skirt. The tired eyes of the people of Skyscraper City were used to all sorts of fashionable disclosures. They were all dance connoisseurs and as such admired her moves instead of criticizing her clothing.

Chapter

4

After half a year of massive fun, things between Vivvy and Chris got complicated. Due to her intense infatuation, she gave up her own rented apartment and moved in with him. Everything seemed all right at first. But as the infatuation lost its intensity, as it naturally does over time, all the trouble with Chris's family came to the fore as a maze of human relations and individual histories, all bundled together under the same roof.

They lived in an old town house from the eighteenth century that had been pleasantly renovated.

The thing that one could notice instantly was the central balcony. Architecturally, the balcony was nothing special. It was the flowers that made it special. The hanging geraniums were quite expressive against the white façade. The discriminating eye of the lady of the house, who lived on the most luxurious floor, that is, the second story, had chosen white geraniums carefully interwoven with red ones.

Gertrude, the lady of the house, devoted a great deal of care and attention to the flowers on that balcony. Having the central position, it had to look good to the neighbors and people passing by. Keeping up appearances was the life motto of Vivvy's not yet legally confirmed mother-in-law. And the one thing that really meant a lot to her were those red and white geraniums hanging from the eighteenth-century balcony like a picturesque waterfall. She always invested a lot of time in maintaining them.

Gertrude was over seventy, but she did not mind dealing with one flight of stairs. She much preferred the second floor to the ground floor. Namely, from her majestic balcony she could look down on people passing by. Both literally and figuratively speaking.

In contrast, the third floor was modest, both as regards architecture and decoration. There were two chimneys hurling out of the mansard roof, made of grey shale stone. This floor was an attic with a huge dormer in the center, rising from the central semicircle bulge starting at the very bottom of the building.

Needless to say, Chris's family was well off. There was enough room for three families, but there was definitely not enough space for their egos. The egos of Vivvy and Chris being the smallest, they naturally got squeezed up on the third floor. Vivvy and Chris were happy about it at first, for there was a central staircase starting at the main entrance and totally separating them from the living quarters of their relatives.

Chris's baby brother Steve, who was living on the ground floor, had married a cute little girl named Alice. She was a ballet dancer in the Metropolitan Opera and Ballet with a decent salary. Basically, that was the reason why Steve married her. He was a painter and used to have a job as an art teacher in primary school. Due to his drinking problem, though, he had lost that job and had to live on the income from his paintings. Being relatively young and yet unpopular, he could not make ends meet. That was the reason why he hurried himself into marriage. Alice knew about his drinking and financial difficulties, but was so happy to be proposed to that she had to say yes.

As a ballet dancer, Alice had a perfect figure and with her pale complexion and sky-blue eyes glinting like stars on a clear night she was a real beauty. Her long blond hair resembled a field of ripe wheat ready to be harvested by a happy farmer. Nevertheless, her character was the brutal opposite of her external beauty. She was a selfish, spoiled, and sometimes evil schemer. Naturally the scheming worsened when things did not go her way. And she always had to have things her way.

One fine Sunday morning she came up with the idea that the geraniums on her mother-in-law's balcony were no longer in the best of shape and that they should be replaced with turbo petunias or so-called *surfinias*. They were the height of sophistication that summer and Alice had a thing about fashion in all fields of life.

Vivvy incidentally overheard Gertrude and Alice bickering on the staircase.

Gertrude did not have to shout, for she had a deep voice, further deepened by having smoked since puberty:

"You have no right to interfere with my geraniums! They are mine and mine only!"

Alice, having a shrill but weak voice, was shouting her lungs out:

"I live here too. I have an artistic reputation to maintain!"

"Go and maintain your artistic reputation at the Opera!"

"I can't believe you don't even know what I do! I am not an opera singer!"

"You work in the same institution, so what."

"It's you that should be put in an institution! You have dementia. You forget to water your flowers. Look at them! They are withering!"

"I told you to stay away from my geraniums, both in practice and in your head, you ungrateful little vixen, you!"

"Ungrateful? I'm ungrateful? You are ungrateful, you old sack of bones!"

Vivvy was hurting from listening to such low blows, but she couldn't help eavesdropping.

Gertrude really started shouting this time. She hoped she could chase the little devil from the staircase with her deep voice, but Alice wouldn't give in:

"Old women like you belong in a home. Instead we are putting up with you here!"

"I do not have dementia and I can take perfectly good care of myself. Besides, there is always Margaret to do the cooking and help me with anything I can't do myself. My home is here!"

"Margaret is old herself! You should both be put in a home!"

"Oh dear, cursed be the day that I gave you away to her, Steve!"

"I married your son out of pity! He has a drinking problem!"

"And you have an attitude problem! You think the whole world revolves around you. Try stepping into somebody else's shoes now and then for a change."

Vivvy couldn't stop herself from stepping onto the staircase, even though her instincts were telling her to stay out of the conflict:

"Ladies, please, your loud voices will cause the façade to crack. Please stop fighting over something so insignificant as the geraniums."

Gertrude did not recognize the reconciling effort in Vivvy's words. On the contrary, she saw it as another attack from the younger generation and yelled at Vivvy:

"Insignificant! Insignificant? My geraniums are far from insignificant! They have a central position not only on the façade, but also in the way we present ourselves to the public. What would others think if we just threw them out, like this little devil is proposing!"

And there it was again. Vivvy had just poured more fuel on the everlasting fire of hatred between Gertrude and Alice. The daughter-in-law shouted:

"There! I said you had dementia. You forgot what I said. I never said anything about an empty balcony! I was proposing to replace the geraniums with even more beautiful surfinias."

"Surfinias might look more beautiful to you, but not to me. I am in charge here! I own the place," said Gertrude, who smiled a contented smile having thrown down her best card. She could not believe that she had not thought of it earlier.

Alice caught her breath for a few seconds, yet she recovered from the shock of the argument quickly and resumed the quarreling:

"And you think you can terrorize the younger generation, just because your late husband left everything to you? You are a lazy bitch! You have never worked in your life. All you have done for a lifetime is to sit around and read books. You don't even go for a walk anymore to get some oxygen! No wonder your brain is in such a horrible state!"

Alice thought that she had finally defeated her mother-in-law, but she was wrong. Gertrude had more ammunition in reserve:

"I get my oxygen on that very balcony that is bothering you so much!"

"Oh, won't you stop going on and on about that bloody balcony! The stupid flowers are all you can think of. They mean more to you than the young people living in the same house with you."

Vivvy gave up. She went to her room and put her earplugs in. Gertrude let out her final display of rage before she dropped down on the stairs:

"Stop going on and on about the bloody younger generation! I had to share the stress of my husband's law firm all of my life. Why do you think he was so successful ..." Her voice became milder and milder until she lost consciousness and dropped. Fortunately, she fell on the stairs, not down the stairs. Having seen her mother-in-law faint like that, Alice got scared and called the paramedics from her cell phone instantly. She wanted to beat her in an argument and hear her say she was sorry, but she never wanted her to get hurt.

The strong paramedics were there in the nick of time and took Gertrude to the hospital.

Chris, being a lawyer who had taken on the family business, came home tired as usual. He found the atmosphere in the house oddly peaceful. He was more used to the daily bickering between Gertrude and Alice. He never paid much attention to it, for it was mild in comparison to what he had to put up with in court on certain bitter days.

When he saw Vivvy cry, he knew for sure that something was wrong. He tried to drag out of her what the cause for her tears was, but to no avail. He figured the best thing to do was to leave her alone and go for a walk while it was still daytime. Upon returning from the park, he found Vivvy calm and tranquil, only her brown eyes were a bit reddish from crying. He kindly asked her again and she started to explain her tears with an air of equanimity:

"Oh, it was your mother and Alice again. They were bickering on the stairs again. Gertrude collapsed. She is in hospital now."

"What?"

"You heard me. They were quarreling until she collapsed."

Chris got scared about his mother's health:

"And who is there with her?"

"No one. We are not allowed to visit yet. She is in intensive care. The doctors say that we can visit her tomorrow. Well, not me of course, only close relatives: you and Steve."

"Holy cow! This Alice creature is really incorrigible! I told her to leave that poor mother alone!"

"It's not entirely her fault you know. Gertrude can be a pain in the neck too."

"Yeah?! How so?"

"She keeps interfering with things that do not concern her."

"For instance?"

"Well, you know … Steve has a drinking problem."

"I believe that does concern her! Steve is her son."

"Yes, but she does not live with him. Alice has to put up with his alcoholism. She needs support, not sheer criticism. Gertrude can be harsh with words."

"So can Alice!"

"Oh! I thought at first that you wanted to comfort me."

"And I am not comforting you?"

"No, you are trying to have an argument. You are not in court, you know."

"Sorry for existing, honey."

"You don't have to be sarcastic."

"Oh dear, do you think that I like the fact that I had to take on the family business? I never wanted to be a lawyer. It was not even my choice to study law. I wanted to be a choreographer!"

"And whose fault is it that you are a lawyer today?"

"My mother's!"

"You see. That's what I have been trying to tell you. She is very domineering."

"I believe it's you that is trying to have an argument now."

"You're right. Let's stop talking please. I've had it with bickering for one day."

They hugged and waited there in silence for the happiness hormones to start working. They were so exhausted they fell asleep.

The next morning Chris and Vivvy took a day off from work and drove together to the hospital. The doctor said Gertrude was stable, but should avoid all stress. Chris almost started to yell as he knew they would bicker constantly. He could not picture how the little devil would even consider not quarrelling with her mother-in-law. Vivvy noticed the bubbling anger under the surface of Chris's facial expression and hooked her hand around his elbow subtly, shaking her head. Chris managed to suppress his anger and was grateful to Vivvy for having prevented a most outrageous thing: yelling at the doctor, who had nothing to do with their family problems.

Vivvy promised to talk to Alice and beg her to suppress her rebellious spirit for a while. As usual, Steve was of no help. When things got rough, he tended to pour alcohol over his wild emotions and keep to himself. He was a harmless alcoholic, but of no use in difficult situations. Truth be told, it was a great relief to be able to eliminate him from the equation. Alice was the only one who could be put on a leash for a while. Of course, she promised to be good, but who knows what could get into her pretty little head on a grim day.

Days passed in silence and a strange tranquility filled the three-floor house from the eighteenth century. Geraniums withered, for no one dared to touch them. Then Gertrude was discharged from the hospital. She was stable and slowly recovering, but she could not manage the strength to water the flowers. Vivvy was the only one that had the gumption to tell Gertrude about the condition of her flowers. It turned out that the old lady, as stubborn as she was, reacted calmly to someone approaching her gently:

"I am not trying to scare you or anything. And we can always help you with buying new ones. But I must tell you, so that you are not surprised when you step on the balcony. And we sure hope that that will be soon. Well, there is no easy way of saying this."

And then Vivvy smiled the sweetest smile and finally broke the news to the old lady:

"Your geraniums have withered beyond repair."

Gertrude sighed with relief:

"Oh dear, the way you were putting it, I thought you were trying to tell me that my little Stevie had died of alcohol or something. Don't worry about the bloody geraniums. Maybe Alice was right."

Gertrude looked very seriously and directly into Vivvy's eyes and said with an air of remorse in her voice:

"Maybe I should buy some surfinias."

Vivvy had to suppress an irresistible laugh. Gertrude must have taken the argument regarding the stupid flowers seriously after all. And the heart attack was like restarting a computer that was now willing to run new programs. She did not totally dislike Alice and her modern ideas, but she looked upon Steve as a little boy and Alice thus was just a little girl to her. Chris took on the family business, so she forgave him for having grown up. She wanted Steve to remain a little boy in her mind, though, like a souvenir of the best times of her life. Those were the days when she was taking care of her two young sons.

Back then the family, that is, the father, who was the only member of the family working, lived in a small cottage in the suburbs of Skyscraper City. Jeffrey was a young handsome lawyer pursuing his career. His black hair contrasted with his blue eyes and pale complexion so beautiful that Gertrude had fallen in love with him at first sight. Evil rumors later spread accused her of having married him for his money. It was true that she had no profession and was brought up to marry a rich man. But it must be taken into account that Jeffrey was not very rich when they met. He was new to the law firm he was working for and it was Gertrude's emotional support that had gotten him far in law. On top of that, anyone who knew Gertrude personally could easily testify in court that she had always really loved her late husband.

Chapter

5

In the meantime, things were getting complicated for Vivvy at work too. The boss did not like the fact that Vivvy and I were so popular. All the other artists at the circus, including the acrobats, which in his eyes were the most spectacular, had to live in the shadow of the now famous singing couple.

The first measure the boss took was to cancel the communal singing on Sundays. Vivvy was really upset for those were the evenings that she enjoyed the most. The stands were full and the audience was singing like a huge choir. They had a standard repertoire and could easily pass as a semi-professional choir. The happiness and bliss on the people's faces was clearly apparent.

"Enhanced survivability" was something Vivvy really had a need for, but she was running low on energy. She felt like a soldier ready to defect. Her stress hormones were reaching high levels. She was sweating for no apparent reason and she had trouble falling asleep at night. When she did manage to fall asleep somewhat early, she would wake up at three o'clock in the morning from a nightmare. It was always at three o'clock, which made the whole situation even more annoying.

The nightmare, though, was trying to tell her something. The dream was more or less always the same with a few slight variations. In the nightmare *she was pursued by a group of criminals dressed in black and with fully covered faces. She was running away, trying to escape through dark corridors, doors that had locks that she tried to open but they just wouldn't. She was plodding through misty mazes, foggy forests, and deserted medieval castles.*

No matter how hard she tried to escape the group of five terrorists with machine guns, in the end one of them always shot her and she awoke from the dream.

***

Something interrupted the flow of my memories from the last period of my life in the city. Herbert and I were approaching the Wood of Aquarius. The fog was gone and I could see my old dwarf village amidst the thousand-year-old oaks. I stopped for a moment to recollect my final memory from my times in Skyscraper City.

***

Vivvy had told me about her reoccurring nightmares. She kindly asked me to interpret the dream. I shook my head, looked directly into her eyes for a while without saying anything. I was gathering the grit to tell her the truth:

"It's over Vivvy. We both have to leave the City. We were not meant to gain any enhanced survivability here. Your dream is telling us both to give it up and leave. Go to Pond Town and I will meet your there when I have finished consulting the old wizards in the Wood of Aquarius."

Chapter

6

Surprisingly, the boss did not demand that Vivvy and I work for another month after having given notice. He was glad to get rid of us anyway. I left for the Wood of Aquarius the very same day, while Vivvy still had to say goodbye to Christopher:

"It's not that I don't love you. It's something else and it's very hard to explain."

Chris was very understanding:

"I have been observing you for some time now. You are right, it's hard to explain. But I seem to understand anyway."

"You do?"

"I do."

"How so?"

"Well, we are different, you and I. You grew up in a family where love was more important than money. In my family, it's always been money and prestige that come first. I love that about you – the way you put people first. But you see, our worlds can never coexist. It's like water and oil. They don't mix. What happened at work just made your decision easier."

"I suppose you would never move with me to Pond Town …"

"You're right. My life is here."

They kissed their last kiss and Vivvy took a taxi to the train station. Leaving Skyscraper City, she felt a great burden lifting that somehow eased the pain of losing Christopher. She was glad he had been so understanding. It was the end of October and they were driving past freshly tilled fields. In the red sunset the soil took on the most stunning hues, which wrapped around her scared heart. She was afraid she had made a mistake. The feeling was exactly the same as a year and a half before, when she had left her hometown. The agreement to meet me in Pond Town made it a bit easier for her to go through with the decision. I had taken some responsibility off her.

After moving into an apartment building in Pond Town, Vivvy had no idea somebody had already noticed her in a serious and deeply emotional way. His name was Felix. He had caught a glimpse of this beautiful young woman, but how was he supposed to meet her? Being shy, he had no choice but to wait for the perfect moment. She was his new neighbor. She had just moved in and was still so busy with her boxes and furniture that she had not yet had time to notice any of her neighbors in the apartment building. She would rearrange furniture for hours, as if it were the most important decision of her life – how to fill in the empty spaces of her new apartment. Old-new actually, but still new in her life. The apartment was relatively small – 322 sq. ft. That is why it was so difficult to squeeze in all the furniture. You see, she had inherited the furniture from her grandfather. In Skyscraper City there had always been enough space for the furniture: in her rented apartment and at Chris's. But here in Pond Town she chose to buy an apartment, thus it had to be really small. She had also inherited some money from her grandfather and she'd managed to save some while working in the circus.

The furniture being originally her grandfather's, she found it completely impossible to give any of it away. It would have seemed disrespectful to her. She totally forgot to respect herself, though. She would get up in the middle of the night, switch on the light and, bent over the kitchen counter, start sketching a new way to arrange her furniture. After an hour or so, she would throw the sketches into the garbage and go back to bed. No matter how she rearranged, there was always a piece of furniture that she could not squeeze in. So she lived in a total mess between the wooden 'relicts' of her ancestors and cardboard boxes full of clothes, dishes, and several less necessary items. She was also upset because she had to eat out. The stove was ready to be used, but she had two cupboards and she could not decide which one to use. Thus she couldn't decide which one to put the dishes in and consequently she hadn't even bought any cooking ingredients.

Vivvy led her strange transitional life on the second floor, while Felix, her handsome young admirer, had an apartment on the third floor. His apartment was a mess too. For other reasons, naturally. He could not afford a cleaning lady, so he did some tidying up himself. He vacuumed once a month, and took out the garbage once a week. Of course, he had a garbage bin, but that was only for the filthiest of items. He emptied the garbage bin when the odor became too disgusting to bear. That was probably twice a week or at least three times a fortnight. He did not possess a dirty clothes hamper, thus he left them lying around, all over the 430 sq. ft. apartment. Usually he would take them to the laundry, when he started to run out of clean socks. He was a plumber, thus he didn't need ironed shirts. He knew how to boil water, fry or cook an egg, make coffee or tea, but beyond that he was more of a 'defroster' than a cook.

As Felix told me years later, he fell in love at first sight with this mysterious young lady. He saw her carrying boxes out of an old van into her new apartment. He smiled like a baby just given a candy, said hello and asked if he could be of any assistance. She was so worried about the boxes that she didn't even look at him. She uttered her hello mechanically and swallowed the second syllable. He did not remain in her memory. And there he stood, shell-shocked with surprise and admiration for someone who looked so different than him, so elegant, tidy, and careful. It was only about half a minute later that he realized that he looked ridiculous just standing there. So he went off to his third floor.

And then he didn't see her for more than two weeks. He was thinking about her constantly, she even appeared in his dreams. He started to get angry with fate for only bringing them together for a short time and then leaving him yearning like a dog shown some food and then left alone to starve. He was not exactly sure which entity to blame: god, the universe, their destiny written in the stars ... All he knew was that he felt a burning sensation in his chest, a miserable mixture of anger and yearning.

It was a foggy November day outside. While this might have somewhat reduced the intensity of his yearning and anger, the weather added to his sadness that came in the evening, when the anger and yearning had worn him out. Thus, he gradually started to lose faith that he would ever run into her again. The day that he was finally almost entirely without hope he bumped into her while exiting the building. He exclaimed with exuberant joy, transforming in a second: "Hi!" She was coming home from work and was so tired that she could not find the strength to look into a stranger's face. Instead she said "Hi" back in a most lethargic tone of voice, so silently that it was on the verge of whispering, and hurried to her door.

He was so stunned that he just stood there, holding the main entrance door and looking in her direction. All of a sudden he was filled with joy to such an extent that he could have sung Christmas songs in November and would not have found it annoying. He could have jumped up and down and not found it childish. The very glimpse of her filled his emotional tanks for a week.

Nonetheless, eventually the day came when all the nasty feelings were back. Yearning was back in the saddle, riding a horse that could have won a race had it not been so ballistic. And there was anger growing like a mountain from the seas like a time-lapse of geotectonic movement. As glad as he had been that he'd finally caught a glimpse of her a week ago, the same joy seemed to have merely increased his yearning and anger a week later.

Vivvy started to work as a waitress in a local coffee shop. That was where I met her upon returning from the Wood of Aquarius. Back in Skyscraper City she told me:

"I am a jewelry designer by training, but I am not concentrated on my profession right now. I am simply glad I escaped from my hometown. All I want at the moment is freedom and enough money to make ends meet."

This seemed to continue to be her motto in Pond Town. Had it not been for the superfluous furniture in her new apartment, she would have been happy and satisfied. At that time she did not know that the furniture was not just furniture; it was her past she was refusing to deal with.

But I didn't want to bother her with that particular truth just then:

"So, Vivvy. How's life in a little town? Sorry to have left the big city?"

"On the contrary! I love it here. It's so peaceful. A lot less traffic. The customers are more modest and nice."

"Have you met anyone special?"

"What do you mean special? No, no one in particular."

"Do you miss the circus?"

"The singing was awesome. But I certainly don't miss our horrible boss."

"What about Christopher? Any heartache?"

"I miss the dancing, not him as a person. We weren't right for each other anyway."

Having given me such short answers, it was obvious that she was not in the mood for a chat. The wizards of the Wood of Aquarius had warned me that I was not supposed to bombard her with the wisdom that they had taught me. It was meant to last me for a while, thus I should just use a little at a time, like a medicine. For our first conversation since we'd left the city I decided not to be wise about anything. Establishing contact after our 'runaway' episode was sufficient.

At first I decided to make myself visible only to Vivvy. No one else could see me. However, I noticed Felix staring at Vivvy through the window. Being invisible to him, it was easy for me to slip into his apartment. I had a very strong feeling that Felix was going to play an important role in Vivvy's life, so I did some research.

Felix had decided to pursue a hobby after work in order to get his mind off of this lovely young lady. He resumed a hobby he had pursued as a child, woodcarving. His apartment was small, so he barely managed to squeeze in the basic tools and equipment. On one hand, the hobby helped him take his mind off the young lady. On the other, the lack of space in his tiny little apartment annoyed him. Thus, he wasn't completely sure his new old hobby would be of any help.

Nevertheless, over time, Felix had forgotten about the young lady to some extent, when one foggy evening he heard the doorbell. He opened the door carelessly, thinking it was probably Josephine again, an elderly neighbor constantly running out of coffee.

"Hi, my name's Vivvy, your new neighbor."

"Eeeee, eeee, … I mean, eeeee. Yes, of course, do come in. My name's Felix."

He offered his hand, but drew it back instantly as he noticed a shadow of shyness in her angelic smile.

"No, no, thank you," she replied and looked down, "I didn't want to bother you. But I've run out of coffee and it's Sunday morning. You know, all the shops are closed."

Felix made a huge effort not to laugh at the charming coincidence and ran into the kitchen with her empty jar. "Oh, I wish she would run out more often," he thought to himself. With trembling hands, he filled the jar, and the countertop, and ran back to the door. He had to bite his tongue three times in order to prevent himself from asking her to step inside again, since he did not want to show his affection and spoil the moment by doing so.

Vivvy had not known exactly which door led to Felix's apartment. She noticed that he had come from the third floor the day they ran into each other in the stairwell. When she got to the third floor she read all the signs on the doors. Some doors had no signs and some only had surnames. There was only one door with a male first name and a surname. She somehow felt it might belong to the man she had run into the other day. Since that had been her only encounter with her neighbors, she had decided to take a chance and ring the doorbell.

A week later it was a beautiful sunny Sunday morning. The first sunny day after three weeks of thick fog. Felix was foolishly hoping that Vivvy would run out of coffee again. He had spent all Saturday tidying up. His apartment had never been so neat and clean since he'd moved in. He had washed all his dirty socks and clothes. He'd even gone looking for them. He found pungent nonmatching socks in the most unexpected places: the bottom drawer of the cupboard in the kitchen, under a rug in front of the TV set, delicately interwoven between the numerous branches of his ficus tree, and other most unbelievable places – at least to him the places seemed inconceivable. He was wondering what he would have come across if he had decided to thoroughly vacuum the apartment. "What the hell, one should really do this every ten years, even if guests do not show up."

Nonetheless, he found it quite depressing to have spent so much time cleaning and tidying up towards the evening the next day, when it was becoming painfully clear that Vivvy would not run out of coffee every Sunday. Suddenly all the Saturday effort seemed like a waste of time. Watching a magical sunset through his kitchen window on Sunday, he felt sad and disappointed. The moment the sadness and disappointment started to transform into bitterness, he caught a glimpse of something most remarkable. It only lasted a split second, but he could have sworn he'd seen a fairy dancing in the red light of the most perfect sunset he had ever seen. He shook his head, slapped his face and thought to himself: "What, am I hallucinating now?"

As Felix later told me, he was afraid of losing his mind due to his overly intense infatuation. A glass of wine helped him sufficiently relax so as to be able to fall asleep. In his restless sleep he had a most reassuring dream:
He was walking through a magical forest on a fresh cloudy morning with rays of sunlight piercing with bright determination through the greyish-blue clouds. Wherever there was a ray of light resting on the leaves or grass below the trees, he could marvel at the beauty of the dew. The fresh dewdrops were sparkling like pearls around a woman's neck on a cold Sunday morning. He could spot so many different shades of green that he could hardly believe his eyes. Following a gravel path, he walked past so many sorts of trees

and shrubs, ferns, and grass species that he could hardly believe that they were not just a mental fabrication. Gradually the path became narrower and narrower. He glimpsed a smiling dwarf wearing dark green clothes, violet boots, and a black hat with dark violet embroidery. The dwarf's smile was so angelic that Felix did not have a chance to become scared of a creature he dared to believe didn't even exist. The smiling dwarf bowed in front of him and made a welcoming gesture with his hand, showing Felix the way from the point where the gravel path came to an end. Felix looked in the direction where the dwarf had indicated. And to his utter surprise, he glimpsed a white lily that had a transparent image of Vivvy's face in the center of its blossom. The face smiled the smile of a thousand angels and her delicate lips moved almost invisibly, just enough to utter a verse that became imprinted in Felix' memory forever:

*"Do not come too close, or I shall perish.
And be not too far away, or our love will vanish."*

He was able to remember all this upon waking in the morning. It surely brought a grin to his face to recall a soothing dream like that.

There was another phenomenon that bothered him, though. There was something that left him perplexed every evening. It was already dark by the time he would return from work and the streetlight in front of the building where he lived only partially and unclearly lit the yard in front of the building. Thus, he could not tell whether the dwarf that would appear on days when he was very tired was just a play of shadows and nighttime hues or a fabrication of his imagination. He did not believe in dwarfs, thus the reality of the creature was out of the question. At that time he did not know that dwarfs were more than real. That was how I started to appear to him and slowly started to prepare him to meet me. After the coffee incident I became convinced that the two of them were going to be involved. There was simply too much tension in the trivial conversation over the lack of coffee.

Chapter

7

Vivvy was quite happy with her job as a waitress. The salary was decent and so were the customers. The coffee shop was selling pies and cakes to go with the warm drinks, thus there were no nagging and bottom-grabbing drunken middle-aged men in sight. On the contrary, a glimpse of at least one attractive young man per day was more the rule than an exception.

Her home was close, so she used to walk to work and back home. One evening on her way home the memory of a face most annoying popped into her head. It was the face of Felix, and it kept appearing all the way through the park, and continued while she was crossing the main street and finally turning left to approach her apartment building on one of the side streets. She could not get rid of Felix in her head. It was a lot like an obsessive thought and she did not know what to do with it. Felix had stepped into the coffee shop for a cup of coffee earlier that day, wearing his work clothes and smelling of iron welding. He was so lucky to have come across Vivvy at her work place that he almost dislocated his jaw by smiling from the heart. Yet, it left him a bit sad and perplexed, for he did not know whether her kindness was just the regular professional kindness of a waitress or whether there was maybe more to it.

His persistent smiling and unusual kindness at the coffee shop during daytime were the reasons why Vivvy remembered his face so well in the evening. While approaching the entrance of their apartment building she was quite afraid of running into him again. She sensed something was going on between Felix and her. Something too fresh to put into words. Something that evoked a strange kind of anxiety in her. It might have been a bit similar to staring at a beautiful but too expensive dress in a shop window one passes every day, or twice a day to make it worse.

Since Vivvy had no clue what to do with this new emotion inside her heart, she decided to rearrange the furniture again. But to no avail. She still could not squeeze everything in. "Not enough space!" she exclaimed just before falling asleep. She was no longer desperate, just tired. Rearranging furniture had become an evening routine that – so she believed – helped her fall asleep.

It did not help the neighbors, though. The lady living right beneath her was in her late seventies and had trouble sleeping. Instead of acknowledging various reasons for her insomnia, she chose to simplify the situation and put all the blame on Vivvy. While rearranging furniture was slowly becoming a soothing habit, Vivvy also started to develop a sense of guilt for ruining the evening peace for her neighbors. This abyss that evolved between pleasing herself and pleasing others was growing bigger and developing some horror to it. The seventy-something lady was the only one to complain. The others did not bother. Vivvy was really cautious when moving the furniture. Every piece was on cardboard, so it could slide smoothly without creating much noise. In addition to that, Vivvy went to bed at nine p.m. at the latest. The coffee shop opened at six a.m. for early risers and Vivvy was one of those people who needed eight hours of sleep despite all the clever statistics and recommendations depriving humanity of sleep.

Nonetheless, all the reasoning could not surpass one big

painful thought – compassion for her elderly neighbor.

Amidst the frenzy of her big dilemma, Vivvy heard a knock on her door at half past eight on a cold winter evening of December. Her first thought was: "Oh dear, please, let it be anyone but Miss Claim! I am not ready for her!" For a split second she heard a soothing voice somewhere at the back of her brain saying: "Calm down and open the door. You will be fine." Vivvy knew all too well that any hesitation would only make things worse, so she opened her door with a shaking hand and to her absolute shock and panic … it was Miss Claim, the seventy-something neighbor that had been bothered by Vivvy's rearranging the furniture every evening and had left a signed message in Vivvy's mailbox to no avail.

Vivvy overcame the shock with great effort only to be shocked again. This time by Miss Claim's kindness:

"Dear young lady! I cannot help but sympathize with the young working generation that pays taxes to support us, the retired elderly. I assume your habit of rearranging the furniture helps you relax and fall asleep." She paused to take a breath and looked to the ground, as if she had been trying to gain enough strength to finish what she had come for.

"Oh dear, how does she know me so well?" Vivvy thought with her mouth open and experienced a strange mixture of guilt and compassion spiced with a few pinches of anxiety about what was yet to come.

Miss Claim, who was a master at making polite requests, raised her head only to smile, nod, and repeat: "I understand." She lowered her head again, said "Good night, Vivvy," and left, dragging her left foot as if it were a bit numb.

Vivvy burst out in silent tears, took a step forward in order to glimpse her kind neighbor again, but could not utter a word.

The night to come she had trouble sleeping too. Whenever she managed to fall asleep, she would wake up very soon sobbing from a reoccurring dream that had something most inexplicable and sinister about it.

In her dream, Vivvy had to look after old pensioners in an assisted living home. She hated her job, but there was one lady who always treated her with kindness, no matter how crabby Vivvy might have been all day. At the end of the dream the kind lady died and Vivvy saw a beautiful transparent soul exit the body. The soul looked like a young Miss Claim. Following a wave from the soul heading towards the afterlife, Vivvy always woke up.

That was the end of rearranging the furniture for Vivvy. And the beginning of living in an apartment that looked everything but neat. It was clean all right, but not particularly comfortable. Yet Vivvy was not ready to give up the superfluous furniture yet. At that moment she still did not know that the furniture was not just furniture.

One Saturday morning Vivvy made an arrangement that was far from efficient, but bearable. She decided that the slightly bigger cupboard should stand in the kitchen next to the stove. Thus she could put the cooking utensils in it. She was not surprised to find that very soon the cupboard was full, which meant that there was no space for groceries. How was she supposed to squeeze everything in? She felt so helpless that she shed a tear. She knew all too well this was a vicious circle. She could calm down if she made herself a cup of tea, but how could she do that if the kitchen was a mess of half-emptied boxes, a second cupboard still waiting to be removed, standing in the middle of the boxes like a terrifying skyscraper. And she was sitting on a chair, crying and throwing tissues in a corner that was miraculously empty. With her head hurting from crying and her eyes all blurred, she glimpsed a dwarf dancing on her stove all of a sudden. The dwarf had a tiny pot in his hand and was singing a soothing song that went something like this:

"Oh, my darling girl,
take this pot and swirl,
fill it quickly with water,
All the rest does not matter."

After having drunk the first cup of tea in her new home, she actually felt relieved. And she even came up with an idea. First she took all the cooking utensils out of the cupboard chosen to actually be used in the kitchen. Then she started taking the pots, plates and other dishes in her hands, one by one. She took a close look at each piece and decided whether she really liked it or not. This was not her usual way of tidying up, but this Saturday, on the verge of totally giving up hope for good, she decided to be creative.

The pieces that she liked she put in the cupboard chosen to remain in the kitchen. All the rest she put on her bed in her only room. Clearly the kitchen and the bathroom could not be called rooms, since they were truly small. Thus, she walked back and forth and after an hour of this sorting procedure she felt relieved that the apartment was so small. At least the bed was very close to the kitchen.

When all the boxes that had contained cooking utensils were empty, there was still enough time to hurry to the Saturday fruit and vegetable market, buy fresh ingredients for her vegetable rice, come home, and finally start cooking.

Luckily, she had some rice, salt, and ground black pepper in a box that seemed to be a sort of survival kit she'd brought from Skyscraper City. She could not believe the fact that her hunger was stronger than the need to tear the cardboard boxes apart, remove the packing tape and take the rest of the cardboard to the appropriate recycling bin. She actually started cooking in the middle of something that looked like a post-nuclear-bomb disaster to her. And how she enjoyed it!

Luckily her survival kit included some dish washing liquid and a sponge. Thus she could clean the kitchen sink and the five sq. ft. kitchen counter between the sink and the stove. Then she could proceed with her favorite part of cooking. She touched each carrot with such delicacy, as if it were a magical elixir. She smelled it with her eyes closed and sighed with enjoyment. She left the water running for a while, for this was the first time she was about to drink tap water. She had always drunk bottled water before. When the water had cleared sufficiently, she filled a glass, toasted the kitchen window, and drank her first glass of tap water with joyful passion. She opened the cupboard again and marveled at the delicate array of dishes, which she was committed to keeping that way no matter what. She had forgotten about the less attractive dishes piled on her bed by that time.

Then she proceeded to wash the carrots, chop them carefully, and put them in a small bowl. She smelled them again and smiled. Then she found an appropriate dish for making vegetable rice and fried a chopped onion in it, added the carrots from the bowl and left them frying for a while. In the meantime, she cleaned and chopped a sweet red pepper and added it to the frying pan. When they had all softened up sufficiently, she added rice, water, salt, ground black pepper, and some freshly chopped parsley, left it to boil and then lowered the heat on the electric stove installed by the former owner and left in good shape. Actually, it was a stove and an oven in one piece. She let the rice stew for twenty minutes.

She set a timer on her stove and started to clean up the boxes. She removed the tape carefully and put it in the garbage bin in the closet under the kitchen sink. Once the tape was removed, the cardboard could be folded nicely and she put it in the recycling bin for paper and cardboard. She sighed with relief for she had finally got rid of the boxes and had even managed to get some fresh air while disposing them.

When she had come back to the kitchen, she still had about five minutes left before the rice would be ready. She swept the kitchen floor and moved the superfluous cupboard to the only room – the bedroom. By the time she was finished, the timer on the stove rang and she sighed with relief, for she had become really hungry by then. She had no kitchen table, actually no table at all, but she had two chairs. Therefore, she used one chair to sit on and the other one to put the plate on. And she also arranged a glass of wine she had kept for this fancy occasion. She felt fulfilled and grateful that Miss Claim had finally forced her to do something about the mess in her apartment.

The only thing missing was company. I told her that any time she wished company all she had to do was to contact me telepathically and I, her friend Izzy the dwarf, would appear. Being too small, I was not able to get a job as a waiter, thus I'd proposed to keep in contact with her this way. She agreed:

"O, yes, I think that is a good idea. When I was leaving Skyscraper City, I had many doubts. But there was also a voice telling me that everything would be fine. It sounded like your voice. I think I have had a telepathic connection with you ever since you left the City."

"And how do you like it so far?"

"Oh, it's awesome. This way I am never lonely. I can always talk to you, when I need someone to rely on."

I smiled contently and she asked me something that had been bothering her for a while, yet she put a lot of effort into concealing the serenity of the question:

"By the way, Izzy: How can you tell when you're in love?"

"I wouldn't know. Dwarfs rarely fall in love. But I have memorized the description presented by the Wizard of Love."

"Well ... what did he say?"

"Could we do it the other way around? You tell me how you feel, and I'll tell you if that's just infatuation."

"Hmm, hard to describe, but I will do my best. There is a burning sensation in my stomach."

"Yes, that is one of the symptoms. Experts call it butterflies."

"And I think about him all the time. It's like somebody has switched on the love radio in my head and I don't know where the switch is. I can't turn it off."

"Yes, that's typical as well."

"And then there's this contrast."

"Contrast? Not on the list. What do you mean?"

"On one hand I want to be with him. Talk to him, hold him." She paused.

"Yes ..." I tried to encourage her.

"Well, the passion is so strong that I am afraid of it. It feels like we will both burn to the ground from too much passion if we were to start dating."

"Mhmmm, this could be classified as ... let me see ... what else was on the list ... O, yes, confusion. Confusion is brought about by changes in ways of thinking and feeling. It's normal. Don't worry."

I was really glad to finally see her smile, for her face had already turned pale from anxiety. We chose to change the subject in order not to get too serious about it. I refrained from asking her whether she was talking about Felix, which was not an easy thing to do, for I was really curious. But then again, I was almost completely certain it was Felix.

After the modest but delicious meal and all the laughs, she spent an hour cleaning the kitchen. First she cleaned the kitchen sink, the cabinet underneath it, and the stove and the oven thoroughly. Then she emptied the cupboard and washed all the dishes. She had to wipe them dry simultaneously and put them on the stove, on the kitchen counter and in the oven so cleverly such that they would all fit on such a small surface. Then she even cleaned the cupboard thoroughly and put all the dishes inside, of course in the exact same arrangement she intended to maintain for good. Order was a big issue for Vivvy. Last but not least, she cleaned the two chairs, the window, and wiped the kitchen floor as the final touch. The kitchen was sorted out, but she still had cardboard boxes full of clothes, shoes, linen, and blankets in her room, where there were two closets, one next to the wall and the other one in front of it, both facing the superfluous cupboard and blocking most of the view from the bed through the window. Luckily she did not have two beds!

Having taken care of all that, she paused to marvel at the rosy sunset, drank a glass of tap water, which she found invigorating, and dragged her feet towards her bed, for she had truly and utterly tired herself out with her obsessive effort. To her surprise, the bed was covered with the less attractive, old, and partially broken – and useless – cooking utensils, which she was not yet ready to throw away. First she thought of cleaning the second cupboard standing in the room close to her bed and of cleaning the utensils too. But she was simply too exhausted, so she simply stuffed the 'relicts' of her ancestors into the less fancy cupboard without any special order or cleaning and dropped onto her bed. She fell asleep within seconds. As she lay down on her bed she thought she would wake up later in the evening to shower and brush her teeth, but since she had pulled a woolen blanket out of a cardboard box in her room and snuggled underneath it, she slept all the way till Sunday morning.

Chapter

Felix was thrilled to find a new job just a few blocks away from the Sunrise Coffee Shop, where Vivvy worked. Consequently, he could have his brunch at eleven a.m. every day and smile at the girl of his dreams. He did not want to appear too pushy, thus he left a day or two per week out, eating somewhere else. Vivvy was always nice, but she was nice to other customers as well. Therefore he really couldn't tell whether he should summon the courage to ask her out or not. His subcontractor work renovating a water pipeline system in a local school nearby was approaching an end. His next project would be miles away from Vivvy. Thus Felix had to face a major dilemma: to ask or not to ask? If he were to ask her out, would she feel rushed into a relationship and say 'no'? In that case he would never have the guts to try again. Or should he simply wait for a better opportunity, which would be vague and uncertain, leaving him in agony for an unlimited period of time? It was a tough call to make.

So there he was, his last working day in this neighborhood, his hands all wet with sweat, quivering so intensely he was afraid to sip his coffee. At the same time, he was gripping his cup on the table so firmly that one would think that this cup of coffee were his last chance. He looked deeply into her beautiful brown eyes when she brought the check and even opened his mouth, ready to utter the words he had been preparing for weeks so carefully ... and nothing. Silence. He could not speak.

Luckily Vivvy noticed his agony and relieved him of the pain of the moment of not knowing how much pain was there to come in the future for both of them:

"Wanna ask me out, Felix?"

Suddenly Felix regained his ability to speak and whispered a shy but heart-warming:

"Yes."

Vivvy, on the other hand, showed substantial self-confidence:

"My place?"

Felix nodded with a cherubic smile, following which Vivvy showed even more self-confidence and her practical feminine side:

"I still don't have a kitchen table. Do you think you could take some measurements and help me buy one? Then I can have you over for dinner. I work in a public place where people go out to eat, so I prefer to eat at home in my spare time. Is that O.K. with you?"

Felix nodded again with even more enthusiasm, his face glowing with bliss and relief. They set up a date three days later and there he was, ringing her doorbell on a beautiful sunny Saturday morning.

Upon entering her apartment everything went so smoothly. He acted like a professional and Vivvy was very practical too. There was nothing romantic about their first date. Felix was relieved. He was not a man of big words. He preferred to show his affection by doing somebody a favor. Yet upon closer inspection, anyone would have noticed the particular smiles on their faces that revealed a bit more than just a professional relationship. They both knew this was not business, for Felix would never have taken money from Vivvy. And Vivvy knew she would have insulted him by offering it.

Vivvy had closed the door to the bedroom, for she didn't want to make a bad impression on Felix. The kitchen was all tidied up and sparkling with cleanliness. The three days she had been 'granted' to prepare were spent thinking about cleaning while still at work already, hurrying home and then performing like a desperate perfectionist in cleaning every single spot of dirt. She surprised even herself with the details she would immerse herself in. The grout between the individual ceramic tiles above the kitchen counter, the sink, and the stove were victims of her cleaning obsession. But she would never have pictured herself cleaning a wall socket above the five sq. ft. kitchen counter. Luckily she didn't get electrocuted.

She had barely managed to wipe the last crumbs of dirt remaining from her last assault on the wall socket when Felix rang her doorbell. She opened the door and proudly presented her spotless kitchen by smiling so intensely that she nearly dislocated her jaw.

Felix, on the other hand, impressed her with his wit and with his stunning precision while taking measurements for her kitchen table. When he had finished with his neat sketches, they went out for a beer. What a relief! It had gone well for both of them. They both felt that they had managed to impress one another. Unfortunately, the 'beer-date' was really short, for Felix was summoned by his boss. After a brief moment of disappointment, they both felt glad that the conversation at the bar had been kept under a minute, for they were afraid of spoiling the moment by saying something stupid. What mattered was that there was now a new entry in Felix's mobile phone: Vivvy.

Vivvy summoned me telepathically right after their date. This time she was sure that she had fallen in love with Felix:

"Oh dear, I am head over heels! This guy is so awesome!"

I somehow knew she had been out on a date with Felix, but I pretended not to know in order to keep the magic of the moment intact:

"And who is the lucky guy, if I may ask?"

"His name is Felix."

"And where did you two meet?"

"Oh, he is my neighbor. I had glanced at him once or twice in the building. And then one day I ran out of coffee and somehow he seemed to be the best choice to go and ask for some."

"You bet, a young muscular guy with a shining face like his was the best choice!" I could not stop myself from giggling.

She opened her eyes wide:

"How do you know what he looks like? I've never introduced you two?!"

I could feel the kind of heat in my cheeks that lets you know you are blushing, so I quickly defended myself:

"Well, sorry Vivvy, but I have a confession to make."

"Yeeeeees?" She looked slightly angry.

"I have a lot of time, you see. Sometimes I sneak around your building. I noticed there was something going on between you two. I got worried, so I checked the guy out."

"You checked him out?" She was on the verge of yelling at that point. "What are you anyway? My bodyguard?"

I stuttered: "W-e-e-ll, I sh-sh-sh-ou-ou-ld like to think so." And then I put on an angry face too, in sheer self-defense, of course.

"Bodyguard? I don't need a bodyguard! I can take care of myself! Stop snooping around and interfering with my life!" At that point she was furious. I had to present my defense quickly and thoroughly:

"I am not here by chance. I believe destiny brought us together. You happen to be a fortress of good will and common sense. And such fortresses need to be protected."

At that point she was blushing. She was too modest to say anything else but:

"Thank you Izzy," and she looked to the ground while uttering those few words. She felt embarrassed for having yelled at me and for having such great virtues attributed to her.

Felix phoned Vivvy the very next day for this was his last day in town. He had to move temporarily due to a new building project. Of course, he expected to be back in a fortnight, but he did not want to keep her waiting for so long, for he had promised to help her buy a new kitchen table. It was Saturday so they decided to go shopping right after breakfast since Vivvy had managed to switch shifts at the last minute.

The local furniture store offered many opportunities to not only find a functional piece of furniture, but also an item that would decorate any type of flat in a nice manner. Felix enjoyed telling Vivvy all he knew about kitchen tables and Vivvy pretended that everything he said was new to her, for she wanted to see even more sparkles in his eyes. Eventually she bought a round, red kitchen table, an item that was supposed to remind her of Felix for life.

Vivvy spent the next fortnight doing virtually everything at the new red kitchen table, the piece of furniture that reminded her of Felix, who was miles away. They texted each other of course, but it was not the same as staring into each other's eyes.

Finally Saturday came, when Felix could visit, and she prepared lunch for both of them. Serving it proudly on her new red kitchen table, she could not help smiling through her heart and listening to Felix with newly acquired admiration for him.

Laughing at each other's jokes, they finished dessert and then, out of the blue, Felix said:

"My place? I have a larger bed I guess."

They ran to his apartment like lunatics and consummated their love with passion. They married the next Saturday, no guests invited, the best man and maid of honor were municipal employees. Despite the insane speed at which their relationship was evolving, they managed to maintain a kernel of common sense: they did not move in together. Of course Vivvy sometimes spent the night at his place, but she was still officially living in her small apartment on the second floor.

I would have been a lot more perplexed and shocked by the intense speed of the love between Vivvy and Felix had I not been advised by the three wizards in the Wood of Aquarius. I remembered the three conversations very clearly. First I talked to the Wizard of Love, who told me something very important to begin with:

"One of the core characteristics of love is that you cannot catch it."

"What do you mean?" I asked all perplexed.

"Think hard. What can you make of it? Give me an example."

"Well, for example … you cannot make somebody love you."

"That's a most obvious example. What else? Put your thinking cap on."

"Hehe, I thought I was already wearing it." I had to giggle. "Well … hmmm … oh, yes, I know: you can't capture it in a definition."

"Very well! Now you are using your brain! There is no definition of love. You have to feel it to know it. It takes on all shapes and sizes. Love stories can be very unpredictable. There are couples everyone says will never make it, but they do. And vice versa."

Having remembered this part of my Socratic conversation with the Wizard of Love, I deduced from it that there was no standard speed at which a love relationship was supposed to move. Each couple had their own speed.

The Wizard of Love went on:

"Humans have developed all sorts of paradigms. That is, they plant some sort of a standard love story into their mind and when it does not go according to this 'plan' they start to panic."

"Yes, I have seen that. And what should they do instead?"

"Love in itself is really simple. One only has to open one's heart to it. Now this second part is difficult: to open one's heart to it."

"But why?"

"Humans have numerous obstacles that stand in the way of love. They can be summed up in two groups: fears based on bad experiences and expectations based on fairy tales in their heads."

"Oops, I thought fairy tales were a good thing."

"They are. But humans often misunderstand them."

"How so?"

"They think their love story has to go in a path that is similar to the way fairy tales unravel. Whereas in reality it is just the point of the story that they should bear in mind."

That reminded me of my second conversation, which was with the Wizard of Common Sense:

"Humans tend to take words too literally."

"Really? Well, let me think. Oh, yes, I have an example. They like to say they need space. And they take it literally. They distance themselves physically. They move away. The moment they are alone they think dating other people is the right thing to do."

"Good example Izzy. And how should they really understand space?"

"In my opinion, it means trust. Asking each other fewer questions. Making fewer accusations. Live and let live, but stay together."

"Here we come to the number one theme: infidelity. They promise each other to be faithful, but they keep breaking the promise. I would say: if you can't keep it, don't promise it."

"True. If a man and a woman start dating, they expect each other to be faithful. There is no promise said out loud, for it is somehow inherent in the relationship itself."

"If there is a hidden agenda, there will be mistrust."

"Sometimes there is no hidden agenda and still there is mistrust and interrogation."

"Couples that wish the best for each other have enough work in taking care of one another. There will be no time for hidden agendas."

"This is not an easy topic."

"You have to work with each couple individually. There is no magic formula," said the Wizard of Common Sense, to wrap it up.

Last but not least, I remembered what the Wizard of Human Relationships of All Kinds (his title sounds much shorter in Dwarf language) said to me:

"Romantic love relationships in general are overrated."

"What do you mean?"

"Love is energy. Anyone can open to it. In any relationship: be it romantic love, friendship, brotherly love, love between parents and their children, etc."

"I still don't know why you find it overrated."

"Humans put all their hopes and dreams into the one relationship: the love relationship that usually brings children and makes a family. But that makes them vulnerable. If they lose their love partner, their world crumbles."

"What should they do instead?"

"Be open to love and let it flow in. It does not come from one's love partner. It comes from the universe. If you open yourself to it, you get it – and spread it – regardless of your marital status." Those were the final words of wisdom I had had to remember at that moment in time.

Chapter

9

One fine Sunday morning right after dawn, Vivvy finally realized that the furniture she had found so hard to stop re-arranging was not just furniture. It was the whole painful history of her family on her mother's side.

Her grandfather had been a carpenter who had lost his wife in a tragic accident. He was an independent tradesman and she was a financially supported wife, bringing him a home-cooked lunch every workday at noon. One fine day it suddenly got dark right around noon. The bluish-grey clouds came out of nowhere and lightning struck the tray she was carrying. The doctors tried to save her, but she was better off dead, for the prognosis was not very bright with all the brain damage caused by the lightning strike.

Vivvy's grandfather was left with three kids, aged fifteen, twelve, and six. Luckily, the eldest was a girl who had been taught by her mother how to take care of a household and her younger siblings. Consequently, Barbara had no teenage carefree years to savor like her peers. She grew up to be bitter and she remained bitter as an adult. Barbara gave birth to only one daughter, Vivvy. Consequently, she involuntarily passed on her bitterness, as the core of her life-view, to Vivvy.

Vivvy, however, was born a stubborn child. And we know all too well how it is with such children who refuse to be miserable just because somebody tries to teach them to be a pessimist and a self-proclaimed victim.

Thus our brave Vivvy rebelled. She had not heard from her mother Barbara for two years at that time – ever since she had left her hometown. Yet she could not get her mother out of her head. The furniture constantly reminded Vivvy of her mother.

In sleepless nights filled with a nasty mixture of anger and guilt, she would beg the universe to show her a way to settle the conflict with her mother.

And one fine starry night the answer finally came. A fairy appeared in her window, approaching as if from the full moon. The fairy started to sing an old slightly melancholic tune and Vivvy started to cry. All of Barbara's lesser and greater attempts to break the optimistic will of her daughter came back in short flashes, finely webbed into a movie of Vivvy's life up to the moment she decided to move away from her mother and never even phone her. The bitter pain that Vivvy felt in her heart while watching and listening to the fairy did not become drenched with a sense of guilt, which was the usual emotion connecting her to her mother. Vivvy felt enormous relief, for no matter how strong the pain was, for the first time in her life she felt guilt-free. The fairy then started to sing a more joyful tune and Vivvy started to realize that not only would she be free from the feeling of guilt from now on, but she also felt no further resentment towards her mother. She decided to phone her mother in the morning and simply tell her the truth, an act so courageous she knew she would need more help from the fairy to perform it. Since the fairy was telepathic, she winked at Vivvy in consent and Vivvy smiled one of the sweetest smiles of her life.

The depth of Vivvy's sleep that night was astonishing. She slept like a little child in the midst of a happy childhood. And upon waking in the morning, even before breakfast, she phoned her mother and told her things she would never have thought she was capable of uttering:

"Mother, I am sorry for phoning after two years, but I needed some time to figure things out. I have forgiven you for everything. But that does not mean that you can go back to normal and control me. I am a grown up that chooses to be happy. I will not interfere with your choice to remain miserable for the rest of your life. But I demand that you respect my choice to be happy. You can hop on the next train and visit me."

First there was silence and Vivvy got a little scared. Yet soon after long seconds of silence something most amazing came out of Barbara's mouth:

"Honey, I am so happy for you. I will check the train timetable and get back to you. Bye."

Vivvy knew that her mother started crying right after finishing, for she could hear her voice breaking just before she hung up. But she felt no guilt whatsoever. Vivvy did her part and Barbara was ready to cooperate, for, frankly speaking, she was not left much choice. She had not heard from her daughter for two years, apart from the little hand-written note that she received from Vivvy notifying her of Vivvy's new whereabouts. Being too proud, she had not tried to contact her. And now her daughter had finally phoned and left her no choice. After a few moments of anger, she suddenly felt relieved, for no choice also meant no opportunity to play the role of a victim she was so good at.

Upon hanging up the phone, Vivvy bowed deeply to the fairy, who had stood by her during the whole conversation, smiling at her, looking her straight in the eye and sending her all the supportive energy she needed to finally set boundaries in her relationship with Barbara.

***

Vivvy's mother-in-law was not as easy to handle as her own mother, though. Being a single mother, she had naturally grown very close to her only son, Felix. Once she even objected to their sleeping arrangements. It was in Felix's flat. She was sipping coffee totally inconspicuously. While talking about the weather and not really listening to Felix and Vivvy, she suddenly raised her voice and said with a trace of innocence:

"If you are pleasuring her regularly, my son, she should at least make your bed and meals!"

She rolled her eyes with pride, and then closed and opened them in order to intensify the effect of her vulgar statement, which had left both Vivvy and Felix speechless. They looked at each other in horror and decided the same instant to ask for a few seconds alone on the balcony, carefully closing the door behind them.

In the safe environment of a lovely winter garden on a glass-enclosed balcony and with all the old useless stuff sensitively covered with climbing plants, Vivvy finally caught her breath and said:

"She's nuts."

Felix looked at the love of his life with compassion and sorrow in his blue eyes and said with a voice so soft one could caress a newborn baby with it:

"I hate to say that I told you so, but…. I suggested that we only agree to see her on occasions when other people would be around too."

Vivvy was still catching her breath and trying to suffocate the anger inside, but to no avail:

"You should have warned me!"

Felix: "I believe that I did."

Vivvy: "No, you did not!"

Felix: "I did too!" Now Felix was getting angry for having been accused wrongly.

Vivvy: "You only proposed that just the three of us should never meet! You never said she was so rude!"

Felix: "Isn't that the same thing? I warned you all right!"

Vivvy: "Felix, you can be so stupid sometimes!"

And that was the moment. The moment when Felix simply ran out of compassion and started to act in self-defense. He yelled at Vivvy:

"My mother was right. The moment you marry a woman she automatically assumes she can boss you around, call you stupid and accuse you of things you have never done. Luckily you still own your apartment. So would you be so kind as to leave?"

Vivvy left speechless, upset and appalled at the new Felix she had never seen before.

Felix proceeded to yell. This time at his mother:

"Mother, I despise you. Do you keep score? How many more? Another dozen? I am not going to marry you, you know!? I really wish you would approve of a woman I'm with some day. I am so furious that I can no longer trust my hands. They feel like grappling something. So would you be so kind as to leave?"

Upon his mother also leaving, he sat down and finished his coffee. He found it very hard to calm down: "Women! And I thought keeping separate apartments would help! What an optimist I was!"

Luckily his temper cooled down quickly. He was ringing Vivvy's bell in about an hour. Vivvy, on the other hand, tended to retreat into herself when attacked. She refused to answer the door.

Vivvy and Felix had thought that the old saying about also marrying a person's relatives was a myth. It turned out to be very real at that moment in their lives, when their relationship seemed to be over for the first time. Some of them, like Barbara, are less married to you, because they do not interfere. Yet some of them, like Felix's mother, are very much married to you. They simply come in the package and one should take them that way. Either you learn to accept the package or you walk away.

Chapter

10

It was a snowy Saturday, the last weekend in January. Vivvy was standing on the first platform at the local train station, waiting for her mother to arrive. Luckily she was freezing her bottom off in the snowstorm, trying to keep her coat on her body, despite the wind's efforts to the contrary. Luckily? Yes. At least the snowflakes in her eyes and the nasty wind made her forget her anxiety about welcoming her mother into her home after two years of total separation. Vivvy might have been brave on the phone, but she could see herself collapsing emotionally under her mother's stare, the serious face of a victim by choice.

Of course, due to the huge quantity of precipitation there was trouble on the rails and the maintenance crew had to deal with the situation. Consequently, the train was late and Vivvy started sneezing. Luckily the train arrived before the onset of another sneezing migraine and Vivvy was actually happy to see her mother, as her arrival rescued her from the horrible snowstorm.

The taxi ride was short and there was no small talk between the two women, so the driver did all the talking and saved them from a premature fight.

Which was totally impossible to avoid once they had managed to dry their hair, change into something more comfortable, and sit down to drink their tea.

Her mother was trying to be constructive, but, since she was new to this strategy of communication, she of course did not succeed:

"You could have at least phoned me. Two years, Vivvy!"

Vivvy got up from the table and freaked out:

"I am sorry, mother. I am sorry that you have to have such a shitty daughter. Really! You deserve someone you can gossip with, someone to share your pessimistic views with. Instead you have me, a strange individualistic creature who will never satisfy your emotional needs."

Barbara was on the verge of tears, but she still managed to utter something identifiable as a sentence:

"Oh my goodness, do you always have to be so graphic?"

Vivvy sat down and started crying. She suddenly felt deep in her heart that two years of total isolation from her mother had simply been too much. But still she could not find it in her heart to say she was sorry.

Barbara saved the moment this time:

"It's O.K. Vivvy. I understand. You needed some time to figure things out. Let's forget the past, shall we. Maybe we could do something fun together. You never liked sitting at a table and talking like the rest of us."

Vivvy looked up in surprise. She thought she was hallucinating. Her mother was ready to have some fun? No, no, this must be a mistake. Not her mother! Vivvy kept staring at her mother, her mouth open in surprise, until Barbara finally proposed that they go to the movies together. She even reserved the tickets over the phone.

It was only years later that Barbara told Vivvy about this miracle. Actually, it was not a miracle. It had been a suggestion from a psychological counselor that Barbara had visited after two years of silence from Vivvy and her own pride. Just another story about the fact that sometimes when we feel that we have really hurt someone and when this is even the truth, we might just have done what was best for everyone. Barbara would never have scheduled an appointment with a psychologist if she weren't truly desperate. For she was utterly convinced she had no problems herself.

Vivvy's mother-in-law, on the other hand, was unbreakable. She would never see a psychological counselor or a self-help group of any kind, for she was perfect. Luckily, at that time Vivvy was able to completely forget about her mother-in-law, for as far as Vivvy was concerned the marriage was over. There were moments of bitterness, resentment, and loneliness, but Vivvy saw them as merely moments of weakness. She intended to drown all her emotions in her work. She started to design jewelry in her spare time. She bought cheaper materials, yet she still managed to design some quite beautiful necklaces and bracelets. She kept them in a box, with no intention of selling them thus far.

Felix, on the other hand, was struggling with anger directed at the entire feminine race for a week or so. Afterwards, however, his rage seemed to vanish faster than the sun just before a summer storm. His heart started to warm up and quite soon all he could feel was love. Love for Vivvy. His one and only. He tried to contact her on her mobile phone every day, but she would not answer. Once a week he rang her doorbell. But she would not answer.

After seven weeks of silence, just when he started to give up hope, his mobile phone rang and the screen announced: 'Vivvy'. They rekindled their love half an hour later and never spoke about the incident again. They were a happy couple again, as if nothing had ever happened.

Felix was very proud of his wife resuming her work that evoked so much passion in her: jewelry design. She had used to design jewelry as a girl. He bought her a book on the topic and she always felt something wonderfully gentle and special whenever she opened that book.

There came a day in April when it was raining so heavily that all the cars had to switch on their yellow fog-lights. The dwarfs and the fairies of the town and its surroundings had the day off. Felix and Vivvy prepared lunch in his flat, for it was Vivvy's day off as well. She had worked the whole weekend, thus she had Monday and Tuesday off. Felix was working on a project where he could take time off as he pleased. He decided to spend Monday and Tuesday with Vivvy and planned to work on the weekend instead.

The happy couple took a nap after lunch, hugging each other and sleeping like angels. They woke up after two hours and instead of whining they decided to put on their most water-resistant clothes and shoes, took their umbrellas and went out into the savage beauty of heavy rain. The raindrops were washing away their memories, angry thoughts, and anxiety about the future. And since there was nobody outside, they could sing their lungs out. They felt really happy.

After a while they saw some lightning and felt they should take cover from it. Thus they discovered another advantage to heavy rain. The store they entered was customer-free, thus Vivvy could choose a bathing suit in peace and quiet. She felt like a queen, for all the staff was there just for her. She selected the most beautiful pink bikinis. Well, at least to her they were something special, probably because of the uniqueness of the rainy day.

On their way home Vivvy picked a rose in a private garden. She was unrecognizable in all that rain gear and she reckoned no one would come out of the house in such weather. This rose was actually the beginning of a new era for the happy couple. They decided to save enough money to buy a small house with a garden. Vivvy wished to grow some flowers and healthy organic vegetables and Felix would have loved to have a small room for woodcarving, a hobby from his childhood.

I saw a burning desire for that house and garden in Vivvy's and Felix' eyes and decided to warn them about wishes as such. I spoke to Vivvy first:

"So, you've decided to start saving money for a house."

"Yes. Isn't it fabulous? We have a goal ahead of us. It's so exciting."

I nodded with a worried expression on my face.

Vivvy inquired with concern: "What?"

"Well, I was just worried that you might get carried away, that's all."

"Oh my gosh, what's wrong now? Am I a bad person if I want a house? Are you afraid our fortress of love might crumble over the dream of a house?" At that point she was a little bit angry.

"No, I am not worried about your love. It's the common sense that worries me. The world of humans is so set on wishes that plans like this can easily blur your mind. You get caught up in a collective frenzy of desire that has nothing to do with you and your original plan. It's dangerous. I am just warning you."

"So what am I supposed to do? Have no wishes at all?"

"No, that would not be natural. Wishes keep us active. We have to have them. It's just that we should control them. They should not become too strong. Sometimes we have to take it easy and wait longer than we originally planned. Sometimes we also have to relinquish a wish, for in time it becomes clear that our plan was not really meant to be. In your case it's a question of haste. Are you going to be able to control the wish and take it easy? To take time and not push yourself too hard?"

"Well, we'll see, shall we? You are too worried. There is nothing wrong with a little haste and pushing yourself to reach a goal."

"Just keep it within the range of 'a little' as you said." Upon having said that I decided to change the subject, for I felt she had had enough of a lesson. I also felt that I should talk to Felix too. Naturally this was not an easy task, for he still thought he might be hallucinating when he saw me.

I asked Vivvy for help: "Do you think you could talk to Felix about me? He does not believe in dwarfs. I would like to talk to him. Could you prepare him somehow?"

"What do you want to talk to him about?"

"I would like to discuss the problem about wishes with him."

"I am not sure I want you to do that."

"Vivvy, please. The house is his project too. I have to talk to him."

"O.K., O.K. I will try to explain."

Having been persuaded that dwarfs exist, Felix seemed ready to face me. He put on an extraordinarily sweet smile and broke the ice for me:

"So, you are Vivvy's bodyguard, eh?"

"Yes," I answered and blushed slightly.

"So I have nothing to fear, eh?" Anyone could see that he did not really believe a dwarf could do any good, but he was really trying to be nice.

"I am doing my best. Listen, there is a particular thing I wanted to talk to you about."

"Shoot."

"Vivvy and you are planning to buy a house. It's going to take time and patience. Don't get carried away by desire. Desires can be dangerous. They are like fire. Fire can be very useful, but it has to be kept within limits. It's the same with wishes."

"We'll keep it within limits." He nodded, but I could not take him seriously, for he still had that exaggerated smile on his face. I did not feel that I had reached him on a personal level, so I tried again:

"It's usually the woman that gets hasty when building a home. It's in their nature to create some kind of safe place for children."

This time he dropped the grin: "Oh, yes, women can be very keen on safety."

"So keen that they create danger out of it."

"You must be a mind reader." That time he looked directly into my eyes and he no longer had that grinning mask on his face. A second of silence and a stern look were enough to reassure me that he had understood.

Months later it seemed like we had never had the two conversations. Vivvy and Felix started to work twice as hard. Vivvy would work weekends, which paid higher than the weekdays. And she usually only took Mondays off. Felix took on more work than he could handle and soon they had a new problem. They spent less and less time together and started to grow apart. They would quarrel more, they had silent weeks, even weeks when they refused to see each other, for they still maintained separate apartments.

They did not recognize their mistake, for they had all the best intentions for their common future. The dream of a cute little house and a garden, a safe place to raise a couple of kids, became imprinted in their brain so deeply and it gradually became so irresistible that they both started to forget about their relationship and eventually their health.

After approximately two years of fiercely pursuing their dream, they each confronted me separately but on the same day with an account of a dream. They both dreamt exactly the same story on the same night:

There was a two-year-old boy that seemed to be theirs. The boy was not talking yet and Vivvy and Felix felt very frustrated about it. They tried to persuade the boy that it was time to start talking. The boy did not understand at first. The parents felt even more worried, sad, and hopeless. The boy recognized the pain in his parents' hearts. He strove to say a word, but the sound that came out sounded nothing like a word. The more the boy made an effort to speak, the weirder the sounds that came out. At the end of the dream the parents started to panic, for the sounds also grew too loud for the neighbors. They started to complain. The dream ended in a panic. The boy got so loud that the police had to interfere, but the sounds were still nothing like words.

Vivvy and Felix both woke up from the nightmare and hurried to contact me as soon as possible for a dream interpretation. I did my best not to moralize:

"The two year old boy is your house project. You are rushing it."

They both agreed to take it easy, but soon forgot about their promise. The same dream appeared a few more times, but their desire was stronger. They kept working like crazy. It was like they had boarded a speedy train and couldn't get off. After three years of working like a dog, Vivvy suddenly fell ill. She had breast cancer.

Felix and Vivvy found themselves simply replacing one obsession with another. This time they strove to work as little as possible and focused on her recovery instead.

Between all the operations, chemotherapy, and all the alternative medicine approaches, they found themselves one foggy afternoon in November, both with a day off from work, staring through the window. They had nothing more to say to each other. No matter how hard they had tried to make this marriage work, it seemed like fate was not on their side.

To their complete dismay, in a moment of deepest despair, a fairy emerged from a sparkling haze. She spoke in a voice softer than cotton and they listened with mouths agape:

"Calm down my children. Calm down. It's time to put on the brakes and hold your horses. You have done absolutely everything to prevent the cancer from spreading from within a vast void of fear and disorientation. It's O.K. to have dreams, but take your time. Who set the deadline in your heads? Who enslaved you in chains of greed? Break free from your expectations and embrace the quotidian. Dive into the stream of your daily duties and daily pleasures. Let your love and faith have no limits. May your house be your goal and not your tombstone. You have to let your love for each other predominate, as the part of your heart that should be filled with love for yourself has turned to stone. Forget about the house for a while. And also forget about the cancer. Go back to a normal work schedule, cook healthy food, get nine hours of sleep, pursue your hobbies, make love, don't fight and your view of the future will become bright."

Since they had been completely hopeless prior to the appearance of this fairy, they decided to do as the fairy said.

You can guess what the hardest part was: the part about not fighting. Oh, they did fight. All the frustrations from the period when they had totally neglected the needs of their bodies and souls came out in the form of rage. They were both angry with themselves, but since they were married it was more convenient to vent the rage onto each other.

Their faith in love being strong as a rock, they stayed together and the rage started to calm after a year or so.

I came over on a Saturday afternoon and tried to start some idle conversation:

"The weather has really been nice. I mean for November, so sunny."

Vivvy seemed to have recognized my intention: "Yes, the sun is really warm for this time of year," which Felix nodded to in consent, but refused to say anything.

We were sitting outside in the late afternoon sun staring at the garden. I said:

"You have some late blossoming perennials here. Very nice."

Vivvy got a bit livelier for it was a super safe subject to talk about: "The chrysanthemums are in full bloom."

I asked: "Which are the chrysanthemums?" I tried to show as much interest as possible, for I intended to stay on that extremely safe topic.

Vivvy: "The white ones in front and the few yellow ones on the left."

Felix awoke from his silence that had seemed unquenchable: "What about the red ones? What are they called?"

Vivvy finally smiled a modest smile: "Those are roses. They seemed to have been done for this season, but they blossomed again a few days ago."

I took a few steps to look at the roses from up close and while walking back to my chair I said: "I must say, they are magnificent. And boy do they smell nice!"

Vivvy sighed: "I'm so tired. Are you guys tired too?"

Felix and I looked at each other and since it seemed most appropriate to be tired, we both said: "Yes."

Vivvy stood up and said: "I'm going to make some coffee." She was so distracted she forgot to ask us if we wanted a cup of coffee. She must have been deep in thought over something. Her telepathic channel was shut. I could not get through. Something told me to leave her alone. She needed e few moments on her own. Making coffee was just an excuse.

We must have been silent for a few minutes before Felix finally mumbled: "She is awfully silent for a woman these days. And she complains about being tired often. Frequently those are the only words she utters the whole day."

I tried to be supportive but not wise, for I reckoned a lecture was the last thing Felix needed at that time: "Give her time. She has been through a lot."

Felix: "I do give her time. It's just that I feel superfluous."

"It's normal to feel that way. You need time too. You have been through a lot with her."

Felix looked down and started nodding. It was odd to watch him nod like that. He was deep in thought; his mind had left our setting. Yet he kept nodding as if it were a motion he had started and forgotten about. After a while I noticed a tear on his cheek. The moment he became aware of the tear, he stood up impulsively and turned away to wipe the tear. Then he returned to his chair, sat down, looked at me and put an artificial smile on his faded face:

"Have you been to the Wood of Aquarius lately, Izzy?"

"Oh, no, haven't felt the need."

"Ever miss your folks?"

"I do, but I have to focus on what is going on here."

"The fortress of common sense is falling apart, I'm afraid. Me included." He looked down again, almost as if ashamed.

I strove to put as much compassion as I could possibly master in my last words before I disappeared for the day: "Don't worry Felix. I wouldn't have to be here if you two were perfect. Nobody is."

The life of Vivvy and Felix became dull but tranquil. They had even stopped checking their savings account when all of a sudden Vivvy noticed an account statement in the mail at exactly the same moment when Felix spotted an ad for a small house with a garden for sale. They looked at each other and they knew this was their dream house and bought it the very next day. Both apartments were sold in the morning and the house was theirs in the evening.

Vivvy was so overwhelmed with happiness that she found it very easy to sell the furniture in her old apartment as well. It seemed like a perfect opportunity to finally say good-bye to her past that had been dwelling in the old furniture for years. There was only one piece of furniture that she took with her to their new house. It was that round red kitchen table that Felix had taken measures for on their first date and that was supposed to remind her of Felix for life.

After getting over the weariness from moving, Felix and Vivvy felt as if they had fallen in love again. The battles were won and instead of breaking up, which would have been the easy way out, they stayed together and achieved a new level of marital bliss, like a gift from above.

The first half a year of living in the new house was wonderful.

The blossoming perennials served as a welcoming committee in a small but utterly cute and heart-warming house for two people expecting a child. Well, not literary expecting a child, but somehow working on it with passion. Conceiving a child became a new obsession for Vivvy, while Felix basically concentrated on the work in progress and not so much on the result.

Vivvy gradually became obsessed with intercourse as the way to achieve the goal: conception. She studied new positions in the Kama Sutra, bought sexy underwear, etc. Felix enjoyed 'the new Vivvy' for a while, but after a while he started to feel pressured and what was worse, he noticed that Vivvy was not really having fun anymore. She was obsessed with the notion that she had to get pregnant. Thus the lust started to vanish and after two years of 'planned intercourse' they stopped having any. They grew apart again. The doctors suggested artificial insemination, but Felix was against it. He said they should just calm down, take it easy, and be patient, let nature take its course. He was simply too tired of medical procedures from the period of battling cancer, thus he did not wish to see Vivvy go through the ordeal of hormonal injections. He said it was not worth it and Vivvy hated him for it.

This time they really got a divorce. Yet neither of them wanted to leave the house. Consequently, they fought over the house in court. A new ordeal that drained the last ounce of energy out of them. They gradually became so exhausted from fighting over the house that they simply stopped going to court, stopped talking to each other. But neither of them moved. Thus they were legally separated but still lived in the same house. She still bought food for both and prepared the meals, he still paid the bills. Silence was their only communication.

That time even I felt totally hopeless. I decided to go back to the Wood of Aquarius for a while and re-charge my wisdom batteries. I approached the Wizard of Love and consulted him on how to fix a marriage that had clearly fallen apart. There simply appeared to be too little love. And a lack of common sense seemed to go hand in hand with it. I felt I had failed in my mission.

The Wizard of Love was very supportive after I told him about my presumably failed mission. He said: "You haven't failed anything. The couple is only going through a very difficult phase. It's called marriage."

I tried to blame it on Vivvy: "I don't understand how she didn't learn anything. The desire to buy a house made her ill. Luckily she got better. But the house came, in its own good time, not any earlier. Now she is obsessed with another desire: a child. She can't think straight."

Then the Wizard of Love told me something most surprising: "The wish to have a child is not really a wish."

I was perplexed: "No?"

"No. If a man and a woman are together and they are having intercourse, a child is the most natural thing that happens. It's the course of nature. Now, in the event there is no child, the woman feels somehow cheated. She is not getting what is rightfully hers. And she starts blaming the one that is closest at hand: the man."

"Oh, interesting. Thank you. I see things differently now. But what can I do?"

"Be a good friend."

"I'm not sure I know what that means anymore. I'm confused."

"Listen to them and comfort them."

"Listen I can, but how am I supposed to comfort them?"

"Tell them it's a phase they are going through. Perhaps they should see a couples therapist. We'll help you with this. In times like this all sorts of mental garbage emerges from the subconscious, including childhood traumas that have nothing to do with the marriage."

"And what should I say about the baby?"

"Just tell them to be patient. Vivvy will get pregnant when the time is right."

Just to be on the safe side, I spoke to the Wizard of Common Sense and with the Wizard of Human Relationships of All Kinds. They gave me very similar words of wisdom. Consequently, I returned to the world of humans with a smile on my face and with newly developed optimism in my heart.

Chapter

11

Vivvy and Felix had got so used to ignoring each other that one fine October evening they were both sitting in the backyard, watching the sunset, fully unaware of each other's presence. Suddenly they heard a delicate melody coming out of nowhere and soon seven dwarfs appeared dancing in from of them. The sheer number of supernatural creatures dumbfounded them. The dancing consumed all their attention and after the seven dwarfs had danced away, they simultaneously turned to each other and asked:

"Did you see what I saw?"

They started talking about what had just happened as if the divorce and the months of silence were not hanging over their heads. Now filled with supernatural energy by the dwarfs, they made an appointment to see a couples therapist.

They saw the therapist each individually for a few months and he listened to them whine. Vivvy would complain about how Felix did not want kids, which was of course her interpretation of his reluctance to have "planned intercourse" or to expose Vivvy to hormonal injections. Felix complained about how the pregnancy planning had eventually ruined their 'night life'. As the therapy got deeper Vivvy started complaining about how her mother-in-law did not accept her. And Felix complained that he would never be good enough for Vivvy or at least he felt that way.

With the worst of mental garbage now released from their mouths, the therapist started to schedule them together. And that was when the real fighting began. The therapist let them fight for a few months, almost falling asleep during such sessions because he was so bored by the typical discussions he had been hearing from all his clients for years. He did not want to disturb the couple, because he knew that they needed a decent fight. He also knew when to stop them and start guiding them to constructive conversation. Many couples could not manage to swallow their pride and they never made the transition to constructiveness, but luckily Vivvy and Felix did.

Funnily enough, the day that they hugged each other in front of the therapist and made him cry tears of happiness, for it was a scene most rare in an office like that, was the day that Vivvy found out she was pregnant. Eight months later she gave birth to a little girl, whom they named Elizabeth.

Fortunately, they did not have to re-marry, for they had not been able to come to an agreement about the house and thus had never really divorced. It is funny how things you build together – like a comfortable home – can see you through the rough patches. You might think you don't want to give up the house, but actually you don't want to give up the marriage. You are simply too proud to admit that. Instead, you hide yourself behind a real estate claim, pretending to be emotionally cool about the love relationship that is falling apart.

I was really glad I had spoken to the Wizard of Love, who had ordered the dancing dwarfs that had eventually triggered the couples therapy. When I made my first visit to see the little Elizabeth I kept those thoughts to myself. I did not want to talk about the past, for the present moment was all that mattered. There they were: Vivvy, Felix, and Elizabeth, a happy family. Breast-feeding wasn't possible, but the baby seemed happy. The love from her parents must have substituted for the lack she suffered from being fed only powder milk.

I complimented her most kindly: "She's a very sweet baby. Calm like her father and beautiful like her mother."

Vivvy exclaimed rather loudly, but still rather cheerfully: "Oh, and her mother is a nervous wreck?!"

I consoled her: "No, I didn't mean that. You are a rather calm person too. I just picked two characteristics."

Vivvy: "It's O.K. I was joking."

Felix: "We weren't very calm at that couples therapist."

I tried to change the subject: "That's different. You had to vent. It was a part of the therapy. And now you have your marriage back and the little girl is a plus. It's so nice to see you together so happy."

"Let me grab a camera," said Felix dashing away. He came back with a camera and took some of the most beautiful family photos imaginable. Upon checking the digital photos after the photo session he was surprised I was not in any of them:

"Is it some kind of magic? Did you delete yourself from all the photos? I'm sure I got you in the frame several times."

I had to giggle: "No, no, I performed no magic. Dwarfs don't usually perform magic. That's something elves do. It's a simple fact that we exist on another level. And no one can take pictures of us. The camera doesn't catch our level. It's pure physics."

Felix: "Oh, that's amazing. I never thought of that. Of course,

I've never come across a photo of a dwarf."

I nodded: "Always sketches, yes."

Felix: "Do you think Elizabeth can see you?"

I smiled contently knowing Felix would like her to see me: "I doubt it. She's too little."

Felix: "Make sure to appear to her when she gets older, will you? I want us all to be friends!"

"Oh, children have no problem making friends with dwarfs. No need to worry about that," I added and tickled Elizabeth's foot. She barely reacted, but we all giggled like little children with a new toy.

Watching Elizabeth grow and learn to walk and talk was like experiencing a miracle. Vivvy, Felix, and I would take time almost every day to observe her progress and discuss her little changes. This sweet girl had brought the couple together like a magnet and they were grateful to life and the universe for her.

By the time Elizabeth was two years old, Vivvy decided to start working again, but only a few hours a day. She designed jewelry and hired a stand at a local marketplace once a month where she would sell all of it; she even started to get orders.

Nursery school was too expensive, thus Vivvy made an arrangement with two younger women she used to wait tables with. Each day one of the three young mothers would watch all the kids, so the other two could do some work. Nursery school was only for the very rich. Consequently, parents figured out a financially feasible way that included the socializing their kids needed in addition to parental care.

It would have been a perfect life were it not for Felix's mother, who had become even more bitter knowing that by having a child her son had become even more connected to Vivvy. Nobody knew what her childhood was like, but everyone agreed that she was evil. She enjoyed insulting people. Insults for her were like food for a hungry stomach. And there was no hope she would ever change. The only solution, and thus the hardest, was to accept her the way she was. The young couple tried to avoid her as much as possible. It was a comfort to realize that their life would have been too perfect had Vivvy's mother-in-law been nicer. People like her mother-in-law remind us of all the others who try to be nice and honest. It is like a storm reminding us of the nice weather. If everyone on the planet were nice, 'nice' would not be a personal trait. If all things were blue, blue would not be a color.

Elizabeth was an interesting child. By the time she was three she could talk quite fluently, but she would refuse to hold a crayon and try to draw. Instead, she loved to spend every minute in the garden looking for snails and spiders. Occasionally she would get so excited over a newly found spider that she wanted to keep the creature in her room, saying that it was her new friend. Her parents never grew tired of gently explaining to her that one could not have a quality relationship with a bug. She must have learned the point already, but she would still bring the insects inside so that she could hear the explanation. For her, this was some sort of a game. And boy did she love to play with her parents. Being free spirits themselves, her parents never forgot how to play, so they eventually learned to love this game as well.

The only problem was the wicked granny, but little Elizabeth managed to trick her into a game as well. A game she had designed just for granny. Felix's mother did not see it as a game at first, but after a while even a cold-hearted woman like her figured the child out and after that they got along well together. The success could have largely been attributed to the patience of Elizabeth, of course.

The game went like this: if the first words granny uttered were nice, Elizabeth would bring her a flower from their garden – if they were nasty, on the other hand, she would bring her an earthworm or a slimy snail granny would be really disgusted with. It was amazing how an egoistic creature like Felix's mother could play along, because the child managed to stay compassionate no matter what.

Her other granny grew old and she had to be put in a home. Vivvy, Felix and Elizabeth would visit her every week and occasionally Vivvy would visit her alone, so they could talk about approaching death and making a 'balance sheet' of Barbara's life. She moved to a home in the same town where the young family lived so they could visit her regularly.

Barbara was very easy to play with and Elizabeth loved to visit. The home for the elderly had a huge garden so Elizabeth would always pick something before entering so she could give it to her granny. Mostly she picked flowers, because this was her nice granny. Only sometimes to spice it up a little she would bring her a spider or a snail. Barbara was just as pleased, but Elizabeth managed to scare some other elderly ladies in the hallway, so Vivvy eventually forbade Elizabeth from bringing animals into the building, saying that, unlike their house, this place had a boss they should all respect. Elizabeth somehow grasped the meaning of it, but was still naughty at times, like all kids are.

There was another thing most peculiar about Elizabeth. She liked frogs. Since there were no frogs in their garden, she would repeatedly manage to persuade her parents to take her to a pond on the outskirts of their town. There she would start to fantasize about kissing a frog. She did not like the standard fairy tale version, where the frog turns into a prince. She fantasized about the frog turning into those divers that she saw on TV who would take you deep into the water and show you all the colorful fish and the rest of the underwater wonder-world. Vivvy and Felix had to keep an eye on her all the time, for she had no fear of the muddy water, which was quite deep at some points already along the shore. If she managed to encounter a frog on the grass along the water, she would scream with joy in a voice almost hysterical and when her parents were too slow, she even managed to kiss the frog. Then she waited for the frog to turn into a professional diver in a wet suit for several minutes and upon realizing that it was not going to happen, she would start weeping her eyes out. Vivvy and Felix tried to prevent all this nonsense, but obviously it was not nonsense to Elizabeth. She needed the experience, all sorrow included. Thus her parents patiently waited for their daughter to grow out of it.

And she did. By the time she started to go to school. School was a totally new experience for Elizabeth, for her parents thought it was not necessary to teach their child to read and write before entering school at the age of six. They thought she should enjoy the carelessness of her childhood before entering the serious world of education. Elizabeth did not take school too seriously, though. For her it meant meeting new people and playing some kind of new games. She was shocked when she got her first grade – satisfactory. She got angry at the teacher and declared to her parents that she no longer wanted to go to that nonsense called school. How can anyone grade you for playing? Playing is supposed to be fun. Instead, with grades the teachers create competition and some kids get really mean trying to be better than you. She despised the whole concept of assigning grades for what you do. At home Elizabeth had been encouraged to do things she liked doing and to respect the freedom and needs of other people and animals and plants. Now all of a sudden she is supposed to do things so she can get some kind of an award for it. Nonsense!

Vivvy and Felix decided to report that she was ill for a few days, so they could really explain the problem to Elizabeth and also to give her sufficient time to adjust. They felt bad about lying to her teacher, but they thought that handling the situation in such a manner would be the best for all. It took some explaining, but in the end Elizabeth was at peace with the fact that most parents taught their children to be good at things and gave them awards, thus the teachers could only carry on what had been started in early childhood. Elizabeth spent a day trying to figure out how she could persuade all parents to be like Felix and Vivvy, but after having slept on it, she decided to give in and adjust, because she really loved her parents and did not want to put them through any more pain and misery.

She was never much of an achiever at school, though. Instead she decided to take over her mother's business some day and spent every free hour helping her mother design and make jewelry. Of course, she did more damage than good at first, but Vivvy was patient, because she saw quick progress in Elizabeth's undertakings.

Elizabeth mentioned her new occupation in school one day and the very next day, while Elizabeth was at school, the school psychologist came by the house to have a chat with Vivvy. The psychologist fervently defended the modern view of how kids are not supposed to be exploited for work. Vivvy knew this type of person and she kept nodding and apologizing, thus the woman left happy and fulfilled. Of course Vivvy was just being polite. For her a thing you like doing was just as much fun as it was work and since Elizabeth had expressed the wish to help her mother herself, Vivvy saw no harm in it. She settled the conflict by advising Elizabeth not to mention her jewelry work at school. Elizabeth got furious again, complaining about the stupidity of the adult generation. Vivvy listened to her, let her vent and then explained how psychologists learned all sorts of funny things at school.

Elizabeth was so cross with school again that she had to extend her visits to 'frog-land' and this time she really wanted to kiss another frog out of sheer desperation. Luckily, they had just had a lesson about bacteria at school and she was a bit disgusted by the idea of kissing a frog. The controversy of wanting and being repelled by it at the same time made her go home and help her mother with her jewelry projects with even more passion.

One rainy day, when Elizabeth was in third grade, she felt very strongly that she should go to the local pond. She found this wish weird, for it was inexplicable. She had forgotten about kissing frogs by then, thus she could not imagine what could possibly be so strong that it literarily drew her to the pond. Upon arriving at the pond Elizabeth was surprised to see especially clear and still water, which had a very soothing impact on her. The sky was covered with clouds and there was no one around, thus she felt as if she were in a private space, isolated from the rest of the world by a cloudy dome. It seemed as if the whole scene had been constructed by the forces of nature just for her. All of a sudden, she glimpsed a little wooden boat approaching out of nowhere. To her pleasant surprise, there were seven dwarfs sitting in that boat, two of them were rowing. The rest of them were singing a joyful tune. They waved at her and she waved back at them.

As they approached, their singing grew louder. Soon they were able to step out of the boat and they started dancing. Amusing Elizabeth seemed to be their only intention.

Having been properly introduced to the dwarfs, I thought it would be a good time to have a chat with Elizabeth. I appeared to her in the garden, a safe space made even safer by the sun setting in red hues. The calmness in the air prepared her, so she was not startled when I suddenly stepped close to her and said:

"Hi Elizabeth. I'm Izzy."

She was playing with a worm and seemed quite busy. Still she looked up to say Hi and looked towards the ground again. I must have seemed a very natural phenomenon to her.

I endeavored to talk to her anyway:

"I'm an old friend of your parents."

"I know," she said without looking up. It was at that moment that I knew she was a very special girl. She must have noticed me, although I had never intentionally appeared to her. I was standing there in silence and puzzled by the girl's abilities when she surprised me again. She threw the worm into the lettuce patch to get his dinner, came back to me, took my hand and said:

"We are going to be friends too, aren't we?"

"Yes, Elizabeth, definitely."

It was the beginning of another wonderful friendship.

Chapter

12

Vivvy could not help but sigh in great relief when it finally started raining after a long, hot, and very dry summer. She could feel all her cells basking in relief and when she looked out of the window to their garden, she could almost see the plants regaining their life force.

Vivvy filled her lungs with air and upon exhaling the phone rang. She was about to receive a phone call that would change her life dramatically. It was Felix. She hardly recognized his voice, for he was on the verge of crying. She had never experienced him in such a distressed state before. Felix told her that his mother had had a heart attack and that he was with her at the hospital as they spoke, waiting for doctors to tell him more about what was to come. His mother was half asleep.

Vivvy felt a strange mixture of pain, relief, and guilt. She could not help thinking that this might be the end of the torture from her mother-in-law that had never let up over the years. On the other hand, she felt very strongly that it was wrong to feel that way.

Vivvy's mother-in-law recovered soon, at least sufficiently to be released from the hospital. There was no room in the local home for the elderly, thus Vivvy prepared her a bed in a spare room in their house. As long as her mother-in-law was weak, she was bearable. Upon regaining strength, she started to accuse Vivvy of being a bad cook, a sloppy cleaning lady, a bad mother, etc.

Vivvy kept meditating and praying for additional strength to be able to put up with such remarks. Luckily they could afford a nurse, who took care of her daily bodily hygiene, but Vivvy still brought her lunch and snacks, so she had to put up with a lot of evil energy from her mother-in-law.

Felix took his mother regularly to physiotherapy, so she soon started to walk again. Vivvy hoped she would become less evil being surrounded by all the beautiful flowers in the garden. But it was just too much to hope for.

There once came a very humid day when the air pressure was low, Vivvy developed a headache and took a nap on the couch. Her mother-in-law came in from the garden, woke her up and started screaming at her: "You cannot sleep in the middle of a work day. You are so lazy!"

Vivvy wanted to slap her face, throw her on the ground and kick her bottom, but it was not in her nature to be aggressive. She left the house in silence instead. When Felix got home he could not get any information out of his mother about Vivvy's whereabouts or about what had made her disappear.

Almost twenty-four hours later, he was about to phone the police. He got a telegram instead. It was a letter from Vivvy, address unknown. There were divorce papers inside. His world began to crumble. This time he knew they were really getting a divorce. He phoned the local home for the elderly and there were still no openings. A feeling of guilt started to eat away at his strength – he should have listened to Vivvy and put her in another home a bit farther away. His mother had always managed to persuade him not to do it. Now he was left with the woman that had caused him the most pain in his entire life. And with a thirteen-year-old experiencing other problems. He felt so alone that he could not recall a more bitter moment of loneliness. It was not loneliness actually. It was the pain of having lost the love of his life.

The divorce went through without any fighting. Elizabeth decided to stay with her father, because at the age of thirteen one's friends are much more important than one's parents and thus she wanted to stay in the same town. Her mother moved to another town to get away from everything. She even gave up the house. She said all she needed was peace. Elizabeth visited her a few times a month, but there was no deeper connection between mother and daughter. Vivvy was distant and Elizabeth felt she'd had enough trouble growing up, thus she could not help her parents fix their marriage.

I visited Vivvy soon after the divorce was finalized. I did not want to bother her sooner, since she never summoned me telepathically. I gathered that she needed peace. Thus, once at her side, I refrained from any wise talk. I had to put a lot of effort into being patient. I knew they would not stay apart forever. Love like theirs is hard to find. It never stops smoldering. Thus I kept hoping and started talking about a safe topic:

"So you are working as a waitress again? Nice customers?"

"Yes, Izzy, they are decent. Listen, Izzy, I'm sorry I haven't contacted you all this time. But I really needed to be alone."

"No problem, Vivvy."

"I remembered what you once said about love. That it comes from a source in the universe. That we need to open ourselves to it. We were both meditating, Felix and I. And this replenishment with love was working. Until she moved in with us. I hate her. The meditation didn't help."

"It's O.K. I understand. She is difficult."

"The wisdom that you brought from the Wood of Aquarius was important and it still is. But there is something even more important, Izzy."

"Yes?"

"The fact that you are always there for me. You are my best friend, Izzy." She hugged me and started sobbing. It was in her warm embrace that I realized the importance of listening and being there for somebody. It's possible that friendship is even more important than any wisdom. For wisdom is hard to put into practice. It's the patience that we have with one another that makes it possible for us to put some wisdom into practice in the end.

Meanwhile, in Pond Town, the years went by, the days seemed all alike. The sparkle in Felix's life was gone. Then all of a sudden his mother died. Vivvy did not show up at the funeral, but she rang him later to express her condolences. This was the first time they had spoken since the divorce.

After the formalities, there was half a minute of silence that seemed longer than eternity. Then Felix swallowed the last remains of his pride mixed with huge quantities of fear and finally said: "I am sorry Vivvy. You were right. I should have put her in another home. She never wanted to go to the local home, even when a space opened up."

Vivvy: "Don't beat yourself up. You could never have forced

her. She broke us up. I blame her, not you."

Then she added with concealed passion: "I never stopped loving you."

Felix had to wipe his tears of happiness and swallow a huge bundle of emotions down his throat in order to be able to speak.

Vivvy knew what he was going through, so she waited for him to speak.

He finally uttered: "Vivvy, I cannot do this over the phone. Could I see you, please?"

Then there came the second longest half a minute in Felix's life. Vivvy did not want to torture him, but she was battling her pride. Luckily after thirty seconds she decided to show her compassion: "O.K. Let's meet. My place or yours?"

Felix lit up with joy and said: "Vivvy, this has always been your place too. I only signed the divorce papers because I did not want to put you through any more pain. This is still your house, no matter what the papers say. The garden is not what it used to be. You took excellent care of it and I am only trying to keep it half alive. I am sure your perennials will be delighted to finally see you again. Please come over. Please."

Vivvy's wish to see Felix again grew stronger every second. She replied: "I can come this afternoon, if you are available."

Felix: "Available?! I am more than available. I have been longing to see you, Vivvy, for a long, long time. Too long actually."

Vivvy: "Shall we say five o'clock?"

Felix: "Perfect. I cannot wait to tell Elizabeth. See you then."

Vivvy: "See you."

An intense pink light entered their hearts upon hanging up. They both found the same picture on their mobile phones and made it their phone "wallpaper". It could have been telepathy or simply the fact that the photo was actually one of the most beautiful photos ever taken of the couple together. She was sitting in a wooden chair in their garden, Elizabeth in her lap, aged three or four, Felix standing beside them and holding his wife's shoulder. Colorful perennials added more harmony to the picture than it needed, but in such moments one cannot find a photo too beautiful, for it is beauty that one lacks if one's heart has been devastated due to years of sorrow and pain.

Elizabeth was so happy about the new developments between her father and mother that she forgot all about her trouble growing up for one afternoon and baked enough cookies for three. She also pulled some weeds out in order to make the garden look a bit more kempt.

Vivvy arrived at five and the three could not stop hugging each other. Especially because Felix and Elizabeth had noticed the small suitcase Vivvy had brought with her by train. They hurried back home from the train station and they could not stop interrupting each other, for they were all too ecstatic to watch their manners.

When Vivvy stepped out of the car and saw her beloved garden, tears came to her eyes. She noticed many details that could be taken care of, but what occupied her mind most was the feeling of being home again. Felix took her suitcase and left it in their bedroom. He would not take 'No' for an answer.

The cookies were delicious, but frankly speaking, they would have tasted good even if they had been burned.

Vivvy, Felix, and Elizabeth had a lot to talk about, for they had not really had a proper chat for three years. Of course Elizabeth had been visiting her mother once a week, but their conversations were really short. Typically, Elizabeth could not wait to start watching TV and Vivvy knew that she had taught her daughter what she could in thirteen years, so she didn't want to bother her. In addition to that, she was too depressed over her broken marriage to be able to really confront anyone openly and engage in conversation. Elizabeth was really glad her mother did not bother her with questions like: "Do you have a boyfriend? Do you know about contraception?" With all the information available on the internet, her mother could hardly tell her anything new.

Illegal drugs were not an issue to Elizabeth, for they had been shown brain scans in school of drug-addicted brain. She really had no intention to make such holes in her brain. Everything else she could talk over with her girlfriends.

Vivvy and Felix, on the other hand, had only spoken over the phone for the last three years and their conversations were of a strictly organizational nature – mostly about Elizabeth.

It was really delightful to see the three of them back together, sitting in the garden, having fun. All of a sudden the seven dwarfs came waltzing in from nowhere, or more probably from the local pond. By then Felix, Vivvy, and Elizabeth had gotten so used to seeing dwarfs that they did not bother to check with each other if the other two had seen them as well.

Later, Felix and Vivvy sat behind that round red kitchen table that Felix had taken measures for on their first date and that was supposed to remind Vivvy of Felix for life. Sipping tea, they remembered their most precious moments together in fast-forward mode. Afterwards, they were spooning and gazing through the window. It was a starry night and it was so beautiful to be back together that they found it hard to fall asleep. Until a fairy appeared in the window, playing a harp and singing a lullaby.

The next couple of years were spent in peace and harmony. Elizabeth continued high school, Felix carried on with his contracting jobs, Vivvy continued to design jewelry.

Elizabeth joined an archaeological group in high school. She had first been acquainted with archaeology in her mother's books on jewelry design. The first chapter usually dealt with ancient jewelry. She found ancient times both mysterious and also quite close, for some shapes seemed to have survived all the waves of the ever new fashions in the history of jewelry design.

Elizabeth's work in the archeological group took on a whole new meaning when she met George. He was a year older and quite handsome. They got along well together. When the group was visiting an archeological museum, for example, they usually managed to find a dark corner where they kissed quickly and then they could not stop giggling. They never got caught while kissing, but everyone knew what was going on due to the almost annoying sounds of giggling coming from the darkest corners. A colleague would exclaim with a sigh: "O my gosh! It's you two again. Why don't you do it here – in the spotlight? We all know what you are doing anyway!" And since the giggling stopped only to hear this speech and resumed right afterwards, pretty soon the whole group was giggling, including the student who had given the standard speech. Elizabeth and George were given a nickname: "the giggling dark corners". The group would crack jokes about this phenomenon, such as: "It's those ghosts watching us from the darkness who find our explanations so silly they have to giggle."

Until one time when George grabbed Elizabeth's bottom. She screamed and ran away, past the surprised group, out of the museum and to the local pond. It was only at the pond that she started to feel safe enough to weep. She started sobbing like a little girl and could not find a way to calm down. Her mind was jumping from images of killing him in revenge, to hugging him and telling him that she understood. After all, they had both reached the age of sixteen and had been dating for over a year now. But the next moment she again felt he deserved to be pushed over a cliff. She felt very strongly that she should have found a way to calm down. She started to inhale deeply and slowly, like she had seen in that meditational breathing video on the net. It did not seem to help her much. Then all of a sudden a fairy appeared, softly gliding along on the surface of the pond. She approached Elizabeth slowly but without any hesitation. She was not singing, but there was a melody coming from an unknown source – Elizabeth could hear a piano playing George's favorite tune. Elizabeth could not help but cry her lungs out again. As she had managed to calm down sufficiently to look up at the fairy again, the fairy said:

"Shhhhh … Don't cry. Nothing has been lost, only something new has been found: a love deeper in kind. He did not mean to hurt you. He did a thing most natural. He is looking for you, worried as hell that he might have lost you."

Elizabeth forgot to cry due to this insightful advice and wiped her eyes unknowingly. The moment the fairy was finished talking, she disappeared. The music continued, though, and Elizabeth finally managed to calm down. She sat there by the pond, listening to the birds singing, watching a reflection of her face in water. She almost caught herself smiling, when another face appeared next to hers in the water. It was George's reflection on the surface of the pond. She pretended she had not noticed him. He said with a lot of fear in his voice:

"I am so sorry Elizabeth. Please forgive me."

And she did. He took her out for some chocolate cake and it was amazing how quickly she recovered from the whole drama once she'd tasted the fine dark chocolate layers and the chocolate mousse layers in between. She was smiling like a little girl by the time she took her third bite and George knew he was off the hook. She was difficult and adorable at the same time. So quick to get upset and also so easy to please.

Barbara, Vivvy's mother, was eighty-five and still living happily in the home for the elderly. Elizabeth would visit her often, for she had discovered that granny was a good source of information. Starting her love life herself, Elizabeth wanted to know all about her mother:

"Why did my mother leave you and go to Skyscraper City?"

"Oh, that's a story for the telling." She smiled with a wealth of understanding for her daughter in her eyes. "You see, your grandfather died. And I exaggerated in mourning. I was too depressed. Vivvy kept telling me that one year of deep mourning was enough. That life must go on. I wouldn't listen. I kept sinking deeper and deeper into depression instead. So one day she packed her bags and took a train to the City."

"But why did she join the circus? Hadn't she always loved jewelry?"

"I guess she wanted to escape from all the family stories so much that she even gave up her passion for designing jewelry. Joining the circus was her ultimate form of rebellion."

At that point Barbara opened a drawer in her bedside table and pulled out a very beautiful amber necklace. She handed it over to Elizabeth, saying:

"This necklace belonged to my mother. She died after being struck by lightning. I gave this necklace to Vivvy when she was thirteen. This was probably one of the reasons why she started to take an interest in jewelry design. When she left for the City, she deliberately left the necklace at home. It was another expression of her rebellion. Here, I want you to have it."

"Oh, thank you Grandma."

They both marveled at the beauty of the necklace and smiled in contentment at each other.